"I have no intention of leaking any information," Lorena said.

Jesse stared at her. "Should I ask for a guarantee, written in stone? After all, I don't know anything about you."

"Do I look like someone who would shoot an innocent couple?"

"No. But you don't look like someone who would be working at Harry's Alligator Farm, either."

Her heart sank. She had a feeling Officer Jesse Crane was going to make sure he knew everything about her within the next forty-eight hours.

Maybe she should just tell him.

Dear Reader,

August in New York City is unique. The buildings and concrete seem to generate heat, people fan themselves on platforms while waiting for an air-conditioned subway car, and reading seems the best escape for the dog days of summer. This month, as I get lost in an Intimate Moments romance, my cat, Antoine, watches the ceiling fan go round and round. He may be contemplating a vertical leap, but I'm thinking how excited readers will be about August's lineup. What better way to spend a hot and muggy afternoon?

New York Times bestselling author Heather Graham returns to Intimate Moments with *Suspicious* (#1379). Set in the Florida Everglades, this roller-coaster read plunges us into a murder investigation…and an unforgettable romance between a detective and a hauntingly beautiful lawyer, who has a particular interest in these mysterious deaths. What happens when a woman wakes up to find she can't remember her identity but can speak several languages? Find out in veteran RaeAnne Thayne's *The Interpreter* (#1380), a love story that will keep you on the edge of your seat.

Vickie Taylor dazzles with her page-turning adventure *Her Last Defense* (#1381), involving a frantic search for a deadly virus-carrying monkey. As a doctor and a Texas Ranger try to ignore their fierce attraction, they plow through the forest to prevent a global crisis. In *Warrior Without Rules* (#1382), Nancy Gideon tells the story of a bodyguard who has his own way of dealing with life: Don't get too involved. Will his assignment to protect an heiress make him break his iron-clad code?

I wish you a joyous end of summer and hope you'll return next month to Intimate Moments, where your thirst for suspense and romance is sure to be satisfied. Happy reading!

Sincerely,

Patience Smith
Associate Senior Editor

Please address questions and book requests to:
Silhouette Reader Service
U.S.: 3010 Walden Ave., P.O. Box 1325, Buffalo, NY 14269
Canadian: P.O. Box 609, Fort Erie, Ont. L2A 5X3

HEATHER GRAHAM

SUSPICIOUS

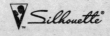

Silhouette

INTIMATE MOMENTS™

Published by Silhouette Books

America's Publisher of Contemporary Romance

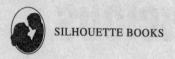 SILHOUETTE BOOKS

ISBN 0-373-27449-1

SUSPICIOUS

Books by Heather Graham

Silhouette Intimate Moments

In the Dark #1309
Suspicious #1379

Books by Heather Graham writing as Heather Graham Pozzessere

Silhouette Intimate Moments

Night Moves #118
The di Medici Bride #132
Double Entendre #145
The Game of Love #165
A Matter of Circumstance #174
Bride of the Tiger #192
All in the Family #205
King of the Castle #220
Strangers in Paradise #225
Angel of Mercy #248
This Rough Magic #260
Lucia in Love #265
Borrowed Angel #293
A Perilous Eden #328
Forever My Love #340
Wedding Bell Blues #352
Snowfire #386
Hatfield and McCoy #416

Silhouette Books

Silhouette Christmas Stories 1991
"The Christmas Bride"

Silhouette Shadows Anthology 1992
"Wilde Imaginings"

Silhouette Shadows 1993
"The Last Cavalier"

HEATHER GRAHAM

New York Times bestselling author Heather Graham has written more than one hundred novels, several of which have been featured by Doubleday Book Club and the Literary Guild. She currently writes for Silhouette Books, HQN Books and MIRA Books, and there are more than twenty million copies of her books in print. Heather lives with her husband and several of her five children in Miami, Florida.

To the Miccosukkee tribe of Florida

Prologue

The eyes stared across the water.

They were soulless eyes, the eyes of a cold-blooded predator, an animal equipped throughout millions of years of existence to hunt and kill.

Just visible over the water's surface, the eyes appeared as innately evil as a pair of black pits in hell.

The prehistoric monster watched. It waited.

From the center seat of his beat-to-shit motorboat, Billy Ray Hare lifted his beer can to the creature. He squinted as he tried to make out the size of the beast, an estimation at best, since the bulk of the body was hidden by the water. Big boy, he thought. Didn't see too many of the really big boys down here anymore. He'd even read some article about the Everglades alligators being kind of thin and scrawny these days, since they were surviving on insects and small prey. But every once in a while now, he'd still see a big beast sunning along the banks of the canals in the deep swamp.

He heard a slithering sound from the canal bank and turned. A smaller gator, maybe five feet long, was moving. Despite the ugly and awkward appearance of the creature, it was swift, fluid and graceful. Uncannily fast. The smaller crocodilian eased down the damp embankment and into the water. Billy watched. He knew the canals, and he knew gators, and he knew that the long-legged, hapless crane fishing for shiners near the shore was a goner.

"Hey, birdie, birdie," Billy Ray crooned. "Ain't you seen the sun? It's dinnertime, baby, dinnertime."

The gator slid into the water, only its eyes visible as the body swiftly disappeared.

A split second later, the beast burst from the water with a spray of power and gaping jaws. The bird let out a screech; its white wings frantically, pathetically, beat the water. But the huge jaws were clamped. The gator slung its head back and forth, shaking its prey near death, then slid back into the water to issue the coup de grâce, drowning its victim.

"It's a damned dog-eat-dog world, ain't it?" Billy murmured dryly aloud. He finished his beer, groped for another, and realized that he'd finished the last of his twelve-pack. Swearing, he noticed that the big gator across the canal hadn't moved. Black reptilian eyes, evil as Satan's own, continued to survey him. He threw his beer can in the direction of the creature. "Eat that, ugly whoreson!" he croaked, and began to laugh. Then he sobered, looking around, thinking for a minute that Jesse Crane might be behind him, ready to haul him in for desecrating his precious muck hole. But Billy Ray was alone in the swamp. Alone with the bugs and birds and reptiles, with no more beer and no fish biting. "Bang-bang, you're dead! I'm hungry, and it's dinnertime. Damned environmentalists." Once upon a time, he could have shot the gator. Now the damn things were protected. You had to wait for gator season to kill the suckers, and then you had to play by all kinds of rules. You could only kill the wretched things according to certain regulations. Too bad. Once upon a time, a big gator like that could have meant some big money....

Big money. What the heck.

They made big money out at that gator farm. Old Harry and his scientist fellow, Dr. Michael, the stinking Australian who thought he was Crocodile Dundee, and Jack Pine, the Seminole, and hell, that whole lot. They made money on alligators. Damn Jesse and his reeking white man's law. Now he was the frigging tribal police.

Billy Ray shook his head. The hell with Jesse Crane and his whole bleeding-heart crowd. What did Jesse know? Tall and dark and too damned good-looking, and all powerful, one foot in the swamp, the other foot firmly planted in the white world. College education, plenty of money now—his late *wife's* money, at that. The hell with him, the hell with all the environmentalists, the hell with the whites all the way. They'd been the ones who screwed up the swamp to begin with. While the whole country was running around screaming about rights—equal pay for women, real justice for blacks, food stamps for refugees— Jesse Crane didn't see that the Indians—the *Native Americans*—were still rotting in the swamps. Jesse had a habit of just leaning back, shrugging, and staring at him with those cool green—white-blooded—eyes of his and saying that no white man was making old Billy Ray be a mean, dirty alcoholic who liked to beat up on his wife. Jesse wanted him in jail. But Ginny, bless her fat, ugly butt, Ginny wouldn't file charges against him. Ginny knew where a wife's place was supposed to be.

Alcoholic, hell. He wasn't no alcoholic. God, he wanted another beer. Screw Jesse Crane.

"And screw you," he said aloud, staring at the gator. Those black eyes hadn't moved; the creature was still staring at him like some prehistoric sentinel. Maybe it was already dead. He squinted, staring hard. Tough now to see, because it was growing late. Dinnertime.

Sunset. It was almost night. He didn't know what he wanted more, something to eat or another beer. He had neither. No fish, and he'd used up his government money.

The sky was orange and red, the beautiful shades that came right before the sun pitched into the horizon. But now the dying orb was creating a beautiful but eerie mantle of color on the water, the trees that draped their branches over it, and the seemingly endless "river of grass" that made up the Everglades. With sunset, everything took on a different hue; white birds were cast in pink and gold, and even the killer heat took a brief holiday. Jesse would sit out here like a lump on a log himself, just thinking that the place—with its thick carpet of mosquitoes and frequent smell of rot—was only a small step from heaven. Their land. Hell, he had news for Jesse. They hadn't been the first Indians—Native Americans—here. The first ones who'd been here had been wiped out far worse than animals ever had. But Jesse seemed to think that being half Indian made him Lord Protector of the realm or something.

Billy smiled. Screw Jesse. It gave him great pleasure just to think nasty thoughts about the man.

A crane called overhead, swooped and soared low, making a sudden catch in the shimmering water, flying away with a fish dangling from its beak. Smart bird—caught his fish, flew away, didn't wait around to become bait himself. In fact, it was a darned great scene, Billy thought sourly. Right out of *National Geographic*. It was all just one rosy-hued, beautiful picture. The damn crane had captured his dinner, the five-foot gator had captured *his* dinner, and all Billy Ray had caught himself was a deeper burn and a beer headache.

And that other gator. The big one. Big enough to gulp up the five-footer. Hell, it was big enough, maybe, to be well over ten feet long. Maybe it was way more than that, even. Son of a bitch, he didn't know. He couldn't tell its size; it was just one big mother, that was all. It was still staring at him. Eyes like glittering onyx as the sun set. Not looking, not moving. The creature didn't seem to blink.

Maybe the big ole gator staring at him was dead. Maybe he could haul the monster in, skin and eat it before any of the sappy-eyed ecologists got wind of the situation. Ginny always knew what to do with gator meat. She'd "gourmeted" it long before fashionable restaurants had started putting it on their menus. Hell, with that gator, they could eat for weeks....

"Hey, there, you butt-ugly thing!" Billy Ray called. He stood up; the boat rocked. Better sit down. The beer had gotten to him more than he'd realized. He picked up an oar and started slowly toward the big gator. It still didn't move. He lifted his oar from the water. Damn, but he was one asshole himself, he realized. Gator had to be alive, the way it was just setting there in the water, eyes above the surface.

Watching him.

Watching him, just like the smaller gator had watched the crane.

"Oh, no, you big ugly asshole!" Billy Ray called out. "Don't you get any ideas. It's *my* dinnertime."

As if duly challenged, the gator suddenly began to move. Billy Ray saw more of its length. More and more… ten feet, twelve, fifteen…hell more, maybe…it was the biggest damned gator he'd seen in his whole life. Maybe it was a stray croc—no, he knew a croc, and he knew a gator. This fellow had a broad snout and clearly separated nostrils, it was just one big mother…cruising. Cruising smoothly toward him, massive body just gliding through the water. Coming fast, fast, faster…

He frowned, shaking his head, realizing he really was in something of a beer fog. Gators didn't come after boats and ram them. They might swing along and take a bite at a hand trailing in the water, but he'd only seen a gator make a run at a boat once, and that was a mother protecting her nest, and she only charged the boat, she didn't ram it.

This one was just warning him away. Hell, where was his gun? He had his shotgun in the boat somewhere….

Unable to tear his eyes from the creature's menacing black orbs, he groped in the boat for his shotgun. His hand gripped the weapon; the creature was still coming. He half stood again, taking aim.

He fired.

He hit the sucker; he knew he hit it.

But the gator kept coming with a sudden ferocious speed.

The animal rammed the boat.

Billy Ray pitched over.

Sunset.

The water had grown dark. He couldn't see a damned

thing. He began to kick madly, aiming for the bank. He swam. He had hit the gator with a shotgun. Surely he had pierced the creature's tough hide; it had just taken the stupid monster a long time to die. He'd been an idiot. His rifle was at the bottom of the muck now; his boat was wrecked, and the water was cool and sobering.

Sober…yeah, dammit, all of a sudden he was just too damned sober.

He twisted around and was just in time to see the monster. Like the others of its kind, it stalked him smoothly. Gracefully. He saw the eyes again, briefly. Cold, brutal, merciless, the eyes of a hell-spawned predator. He saw the head, the long jaws. Biggest damn head he'd ever seen. Couldn't be real.

The eyes slipped beneath the surface.

Billy Ray started to scream. He felt more sober than he had ever felt in his life. Felt everything perfectly clearly.

Felt the movement in the water, the rush beneath him…

He screamed and screamed and screamed. Until the giant jaws snapped shut on him. He felt the excruciating, piercing pain. Then he ceased to scream as the razor-sharp teeth pierced his rib cage, lungs and windpipe.

The creature began to toss its massive head, literally shaking its prey into more easily digestible pieces.

The giant gator sank beneath the surface.

And more of Billy Ray's bones began to crunch….

Billy Ray had been right all along.

It was dinnertime.

Chapter 1

At first it seemed that the sound of the siren wasn't even penetrating the driver's mind.

Either that, or the Lexus intended to race him all the way across the lower portion of the state to the city of Naples, Jesse Crane thought irritably.

It was natural to speed out here—it felt like one of the world's longest, strangest drives, with mile after mile of grass and muck and canal, interspersed by a gas station or tackle shop here or there, the airboat rides, and the Miccosukee camps.

But after you passed the casino, heading west, traces of civilization became few and far between. Despite that, the road was a treacherous one. Impatient drivers trying to pass had caused many a traffic fatality.

He overlooked it when someone seemed competent and was going a rational number of miles over the limit.

But this Lexus…

At last the driver seemed to become aware that he was trailing, the siren blazing. The Lexus pulled over on the embankment.

As Jesse pulled his cruiser off on the shoulder, he saw a blond head dipping—the occupant was obviously searching for the registration. *Or a gun?* There were plenty of toughs who made it out to this section of the world, because there was enough godforsaken space out here for all manner of things to go on. He trod carefully. He was a man who always trod carefully.

As he approached the car, the window came down and a blond head appeared. He was startled, faltering for a fraction of a second.

The woman was stunning. Not just attractive. Stunning. She had the kind of golden beauty that was almost spellbinding. Blond hair that caught the daylight. Delicate features. Huge eyes that reflected a multitude of colors: green, brown, rimmed with gray. Sweeping lashes. Full lips, colored in shell-pink gloss. Perfect for her light complexion and hair.

"Was I speeding?" She sounded as if he were merely a distraction in her important life.

Yeah, the kind of beauty that was almost *spellbinding. But there was also something about her that was irritating as hell!*

The soft sound of a splash drew his attention. Her head jerked around, and she shuddered as they both looked toward the canal. A small alligator had left its sunning spot on the high mud and slipped into the water.

Then she turned back to him and gave him her full attention. She studied him for a moment. "Is this…a joke?"

"No, ma'am. No joke," he said curtly. "License and registration, please."

"Was I speeding?" she asked again, and her seriousness was well done, especially after her earlier remark.

"Speeding? Oh, yeah," he said. "License and registration, please."

"Surely I wasn't going that fast," she said. She was staring at him, not distracted anymore, and frowning. "Are you really a cop?" she demanded suddenly.

"Yes."

She twisted around. "That's not a Metro-Dade car."

"No, I'm not Metro-Dade."

"Then—"

"Miccosukee. Indian police," he said curtly.

"Indian police?" she said, and looked back to him. His temper rose. He felt as if he might as well have said *play* police, or *pretend* police.

"This is my jurisdiction," he said curtly. "One more time. License and registration."

She gritted her teeth, staring at him, antagonism replacing the curiosity in her eyes. Then, every movement irate, she dug into the glove compartment. "Registration," she snapped, handing him the document.

"And license," he said politely.

"Yes, of course. I need to get it."

"Do you know how fast you were going?"

"Um…not that far over the speed limit, surely?"

"Way over," he told her. "See that sign? It says fifty-five. You were topping that by thirty miles an hour."

"I'm sorry," she said. "It didn't feel like I was going that fast."

She dug in her handbag, which was tightly packed and

jumbled, in contrast to the businesslike appearance of the pale blue jacket she wore over a tailored shirt. He began writing the ticket. She produced her license. He kept writing. Her fingers, long, elegant, curled tightly around the steering wheel. "I don't know what's waiting for you in Naples, Miss Fortier, but it's not worth dying for. And if you're not worried about killing yourself, try to remember that you could kill someone else. Slow down on this road."

"I still don't believe I was going that fast," she murmured.

"Trust me, you were," he assured her curtly. He didn't know why she was getting beneath his skin to such a degree. She was passing through. Lots of people tried to speed their way through, east to west, west to east, completely careless of their surroundings, immune to the fact that the populations of Seminoles and Miccosukees in the area might be small, but they existed.

And their lives were as important as any others.

"Fine, then," she murmured, as if barely aware of him, just anxious to be on her way.

"Hey!" He demanded her attention.

She blinked, staring at him. She definitely seemed distracted. And yet, when she stared at him, it was with a strange interest. As if she wanted to listen but somehow couldn't.

"Slow down," he repeated softly and firmly.

She nodded curtly and reached out, accepting her license and registration back, along with the ticket he had written.

Then she shook her head slightly, trying to control her temper. "Thanks," she muttered.

"I'm a real cop, and it's a real ticket, Ms. Fortier."

"Yes, thank you. I'll pay it, with real money," she said sweetly.

He forced a grim smile in return. *Spoiled little rich girl, heading from the playgrounds of Miami Beach to the playgrounds of the western coast of the state.*

He tipped his hat, grateful that she couldn't know what he was thinking. His sunglasses were darkly tinted, well able to hide his thoughts. "Good day, Miss Fortier."

He turned to leave.

"Jerk!" he heard her mutter.

He stiffened, straightened, turned back.

"Pardon? Did you say something?" he asked politely.

She forced a smile. "I said good day to you, too, Officer."

"That's what I thought you said," he told her, turning to go. "Bitch," he murmured beneath his breath.

Or, at least, he thought he'd murmured beneath his breath.

"What did you say?" she demanded sharply.

He turned back. "I said we should both have a lovely day. One big old wonderful, lovely day. Take care, Ms. Fortier."

He proceeded back to his car.

The Lexus slid back onto the road.

He followed it for a good twenty miles. And she knew it. She drove the speed limit.

Not a mile under.

Not a mile over.

The dash phone buzzed softly. He hit the answer button. "Hey, Chief. What's up? Some good ol' boy beating up on his wife again?" He spoke evenly, hoping that was all it was. Too often, out here, it was something else. Something that seldom had to do with his people, his work. The Everglades was a beautiful place for those who loved nature, but pure temptation for those who chose to commit certain crimes.

Over the distance, Emmy sighed. "Nope, just a call from Lars. He wants you to have lunch with him at the new fish place just east of the casino next Friday."

"Tell him sure," Jesse said. "See you soon. Time for me to call it a day."

Clayton Harrison's place was just up ahead. The driveway wasn't easily discernible from the trail, but Jesse knew right where it was. He took a sharp left, turned around and headed back.

He was certain that, as he did so, the Lexus once again picked up speed.

Lorena Fortier set down her pen, sighed, stood and stretched. She left her desk and walked to the door that led out to the hallway in the staff quarters of Harry's Alligator Farm and Museum. She hesitated, looked both ways, then walked down the shadowy hallway. Dim night-lights showed the signs on the various doors she passed.

Her second full day on the job. And her second day of living a deception. She thought about Naples and Marco Island. If only one of those lovely beach communities had been her destination.

She felt herself bristling again as she remembered being stopped the day before by the Miccosukee officer. She had been speeding, and she should have slowed down. It was just that her mind had been racing, and her foot had apparently gone along with it.

And the man who had stopped her…

She felt an odd little tremor shoot through her. He'd just been so startling, and then even a little frightening. For the good or bad, she couldn't remember anyone who had made such an impression on her in a long time. His appearance had been so striking, not at all what she expected from a police officer.

She had apparently made an impression on him, as well. *Rich bitch, no care for anything local...*

She gave herself a shake. Forget it! Move on. Concentrate on the matter at hand!

Large letters on the third door down read Dr. Michael Preston, Research.

She hesitated, then tried the knob. The door, as she had expected, was locked. She slipped her hand into the pocket of her lab coat, curling her fingers around the small lock pick she carried. She was about to work the door open when she heard voices coming from the far end of the hallway.

"So how are the tours going, Michael?" It was her new boss, Harry Rogers, speaking. He was a huge man, with a smile as wide as his belly.

Dr. Michael Preston replied with forced enthusiasm. "Great!"

"I know that you're a researcher, Michael, but part of my dream here is to educate people about reptiles."

"I don't mind the tours. I think I'm pretty good at conveying what we're doing."

Okay, so what did she do now? Lorena wondered. She was new at this whole secret-investigation thing. Should she run back down the hall and into her own office? Or should she bluff it out, walk on down the hall to meet the two of them and ask some kind of lame question?

Running would be insane. They might see her. She would have to bluff.

"Harry, Dr. Preston!" she called, smiling and starting toward them.

"You're the boss, but she calls you 'Harry,' while I'm 'Dr. Preston,'" Michael said to Harry with a groan.

"She knows she can trust me," Harry said, grinning. "She's the new girl on the block—she can't tell yet if you're a dangerously handsome devil, or simply an innocent charmer, a true bookworm."

Lorena laughed softly. "Which is it, Dr. Preston? Are you a devil in disguise? Or a man who is totally trustworthy?" she asked. He was a striking man, not bookish in appearance in the least, considering his reputation as a dedicated researcher, completely passionate about his work. The man was actually the epitome of "tall, dark and handsome," with a wicked grin that could easily seduce a woman into trusting him.

She didn't like the sound of her own laugh, or her question. She tended to be forthright; she wasn't a flirt or a tease, and acting like a coquette felt ridiculous.

But, as she was learning, Dr. Preston was aware of his looks, and more than willing to make use of his natural charm.

He turned it on her now, smiling in her direction, even though he directed his questions to their boss. "What about the lovely Ms. Fortier? Our mystery woman, a glorious golden-haired beauty suddenly landing in this small oasis in the middle of a swamp. Can she be totally trustworthy?" he asked Harry. "Or has she come to seduce our secrets out of us?"

"Well, whatever secrets I have aren't too fascinating, son," Harry said apologetically.

"And I'm afraid my mystery life is rather dull, as well," Lorena said sweetly.

"Were you looking for me?" Harry asked.

"Um…yes. You told me that you had a small gym for

the employees. I thought I would take a look at it. If you could just direct me…"

"The gym is just past the holding pens. Be careful in the dark. The pens are walled, but you don't want to go getting curious, try to bend over the walls and fall in, you know. My gators are well fed, but they're wild animals, after all. And even though I've got security out there, the guards patrol, and with gators, help can never come fast enough."

"I know to be careful, Harry. Thanks." She flashed them both a smile and turned away, feeling frustrated. Did Preston sleep in his lab?

She returned to her room and changed into bike shorts and a tank top. When she left her room again, she could still hear Harry and Michael talking. They were in Preston's lab.

Maybe the gym wasn't such a bad idea, after all.

She left the staff area and started across the huge compound. There were hundreds of gators here, in various stages of growth. Then there was the special pen with Old Elijah. He was huge, a good fifteen feet. He was never part of any show; he was just there for visitors to look at. Next to him were Pat and Darien, both of them adolescents, five feet in length, the gators that were wrestled for the amusement of the crowds.

Jack Pine, a tall, well-muscled Seminole, was standing by the pens with Hugh Humphrey, a wiry blond handler from Australia. Hugh had experience with Outback crocs, and Harry valued having him. When she walked over, the two men were talking quietly with a tall, white-haired man and a veritable giant.

The white-haired man said goodbye, starting away before Lorena got close enough to be introduced to him.

The big man followed. He seemed to grunt, kind of like the alligators, but she assumed that was his way of saying goodbye.

"Ms. Fortier!" Hugh called to her, seeing her as he turned away from the pair who were leaving.

"Hi there!" she called back as she crossed over to the western arc of the building complex. "Who was that?" she asked.

"Who was who?" Hugh asked.

"The men who just left. Do they work here?"

"No, no. They do work for Harry now and then, but they're totally independent. The old guy is Dr. Thiessen, a local vet, and the Neanderthal is the doc's assistant, John Smith. I should have had Doc stay to meet you, but I didn't see you, and he's always busy. He just checks in with us now and then. Doc Thiessen is a hero among the local kids—he's the only guy out there who can really treat a sick turtle or a ball python. You'll meet him soon enough, I wager. He's something. Also knows cattle, gators—and dogs and cats."

"Ah," she murmured. "The big guy is kind of…big."

"Creepy, is that what you mean?" Hugh asked with a laugh.

"No, just…big."

"And dumb. But he's a good worker. Thiessen needs someone like that. He works with some big animals."

"That's certainly understandable. You guys work with some big animals, too," she reminded them.

Hugh offered a grin. "But we're fit and muscled—perfect specimens of manhood. You're supposed to notice that."

She laughed. "You're both in great shape."

"Thanks," Jack Pine offered. "You're welcome to go on about us if you want, but…how are you enjoying the work so far?"

"So far, things have been quite easy. I know you need a nurse on staff, but I haven't even had to deal with a skinned knee yet."

"But you like the place all right?" Hugh asked.

"Yes, just fine."

"A lot of women would find it incredibly weird," Jack told her, inclining his head in a way that made her feel special. Like Preston, he was an intriguing man. Unlike Preston, there didn't seem to be anything cerebral about the attraction. His hair was dark and slick, his eyes nearly as black as his hair; he was bronzed and built—just as he had said. She had liked him instantly—but warily, as well.

He had proudly shown her when they'd met that he'd lost the pinkie finger on his left hand to a gator when he'd learned to wrestle the big reptiles as a boy growing up at Big Cypress Reservation. He seemed to be fearless.

"I like animals," she said.

"These guys are hardly cute and cuddly," Hugh remarked. As if they'd heard him, a number of the alligators set up a racket. They made the strangest noise, as if they were pigs grunting. The cacophony was eerie. She shivered, then thought about the animal's deadly jaws.

She thought about her reasons for being here. Whether she liked the guys who worked here or not, she had to remember to be wary.

She shivered again, suddenly uneasy about being with either man around the prehistoric predators.

Come to think of it, she thought, *she didn't want to be here at all, not at all.*

But she had to be. It was that simple. She had to be.

"You both seem to like gators a lot," she said.

Hugh shrugged. "Well, I made a good living off crocs, so I figure I can make a good living off their cousins, too."

"Like 'em? Hell, no. Respect 'em? Hell, yes," Jack said with a shrug. "But if you're going to work with them, you need to know them. And I can definitely say I know them. I was born and bred in the swamp, so I knew about gators long before I knew about lions, tigers and bears." He grinned and shrugged. "But you, young lady, need to remember a few things that will be important if you ever get in trouble down here. Never get closer than fifteen feet to one of these suckers. And if he's hissing, back away slowly and get the hell away."

"And if you can't get away, make sure you get your weight on its back and push down hard on the nose. It's the top jaw that exerts the pressure. The lower jaw is pretty much worthless," Hugh said.

"I don't intend to get that close to any of them," she assured the men. "You're right—alligators definitely aren't cuddly, but so far, I like this place a lot. I seem to be working with great people," she said, forcing herself to sound nonchalant. They were giving her friendly warnings, nothing more. Despite the grunts from the creatures, which seemed more eerie and foreboding by the moment, she couldn't scream and run away.

"Why, shucks, thanks, ma'am," Hugh teased.

"Thank you both, and good night. See you guys in the morning."

She walked away. She could have sworn she heard the man whisper in her wake. Her skin crawled as she wondered what they were saying.

She entered the gym feeling winded, gasping for breath, though she hadn't walked far at all. She didn't want to work out; she wanted to lock herself into her room. Still, in case she was being followed or watched, she had to act normal. She'd come here to work out, so that was what she would do. She walked to an Exercycle, crawled on and pedaled away.

Fifteen minutes was enough for the night.

She exited the employee gym, more tired from feeling nervous than from her workout. She opened the door a crack, then paused, looking out.

There was a man in the compound. He was standing between two of the alligator pens, hands on hips. At first he was very still, nothing but a dark silhouette in the moonlight. He was tall, broad-shouldered, yet lithe-looking, somehow exuding energy, even in his stillness. He stood in plain view; then he walked around one of the pens, and she noticed that he moved with a sure, fluid stride that was both graceful and, somehow, menacing. Dangerous.

And oddly familiar.

It was her mind tonight, she thought. Everyone she saw seemed furtive, dangerous.

He might just be the security guard. There were several of them, she knew. And, she had been assured, their backgrounds had been checked out by the same careful procedures that casinos used.

No. This man wasn't a security guard. Somehow she knew it.

As he moved and her eyes became more accustomed to the shadows, she could see him more clearly.

He was in black jeans and a black T-shirt. The short sleeves were rolled, and in the moonlight, she could see the bulge of his arm muscles beneath the rolled cotton. His hair was on the long side, sleek, touching his shoulders. Very dark.

The cop! It was the Indian cop who had given her the ticket!

He turned toward the gym suddenly, as if he knew he was being watched. He couldn't, of course. The light was out. He had no way to know the door was open even a crack.

She continued to study him from her safe distance, trying to determine just what made him so imposing and unique.

His features were compelling. Hardened, fascinating. He was a combination of Indian, white and God knew what else. His skin was bronzed, his cheekbones broad, his chin square, like that of a man who knew where he was going—and where he had been. His nose was slightly crooked, as if it might have been broken at some time. She couldn't make out the color of his eyes against the darkness of his hair and the bronze of his flesh. He couldn't possibly see her; still, she felt as if he was staring right through her. She almost stepped back, feeling as if she had been physically touched, as if a rush of smoke and fire had swept through her.

"Jesse," a soft feminine voice said from behind her.

She gasped, then spun around. Sally Dickerson, the head cashier and bookkeeper, was standing behind her. In her early thirties, she was an attractive redhead. Harry said she had a temper, a way with men, and one heck of a way with numbers that had dollar signs attached to them.

"Sorry, you startled me," Lorena said.

Sally glanced at her, and she realized the woman hadn't even heard her gasp. Her attention had been on the man in the moonlight.

"No, *I'm* sorry—I came in the back way, and I didn't realize you hadn't heard me." She was still staring at the man and didn't offer anything more.

"Jesse?" Lorena pressed lightly.

Sally's eyes flicked her way, and the woman smiled broadly. "Yeah, Jesse. He's a cop. A local cop. On the Miccosukee force. He hasn't been back long."

"Oh, I realize that he's a cop," Lorena murmured, wondering if Sally could hear the slight note of bitterness in her tone. "But…he's back from where?"

"Oh…the city. He's something, huh?"

Lorena turned back to study the man in question. Sally didn't need an answer.

Yes, something. He seemed to be both pure grace and pure menace. Powerful, smooth. Sensual, she thought, with some embarrassment. In a thousand years, she never would have admitted that she understood exactly what Sally meant.

No, no, no, no. He was definitely a man with an attitude, and that attitude definitely contained an element of disdain for her. She shook her head slightly, mentally emitting an oath. It now seemed likely that she would meet him again.

Apparently, he hung out around here. And that made him…suspicious.

Cops had been known to be dirty, dirtier even than other men. Sometimes they needed money. Sometimes even good men went bad, seeing how the rich could buy good lawyers and get away with all kinds of things. They had more chance to abuse power, to sneak around, to bribe…

To threaten.

To kill?

"Interesting. We have security guards. Why is he here?" Lorena asked, looking at Sally once again.

"He checks in now and then, makes sure everything is running smoothly."

"Why did he come back?" she asked.

"Oh," Sally said slowly, "his wife was murdered. He was devastated."

"How horrible."

"I know. Damn, I have a busy night ahead of me…but still… Jesse. Excuse me, will you, honey? I want to talk to the man."

"Sure…friends help when you're devastated," Lorena said pleasantly.

Sally shot her a quick glance. "Honey, I said he was devastated, not dead. Take another look at the man, will you?" She opened the door fully and exited the gym. With a sway of her hips, she approached him, calling his name. He turned to her, arching a brow, acknowledging her presence. Sally went straight to him, placing her hands on his chest. She said something softly. He lowered his head, grinning, and the two turned to walk toward the staff quarters.

When they were gone, Lorena left the gym and hurried back across the compound. The alligators began to grunt in a wild, staccato song.

She let herself into her own room, closed and locked the door. She was breathing too heavily once again.

Maybe she was the wrong woman for this job.

No, there was no maybe about it, but that didn't matter. She had to become the right woman, and she would.

She showered, slipped into a nightgown, and assured herself once again that her door was securely locked. Even then, she also checked once more on the small Smith & Wesson she carried. It was loaded, safety on, but close at hand in the top drawer of the nightstand next to the bed. She took one last look at it before she lay down to sleep.

Despite that, she dreamed.

She didn't want to have nightmares; she didn't want to toss and turn. She dreamed far too often of horrible things. She knew that dreams were often extensions of the day's worries, and she *was* constantly worried.

But that night, she didn't dream horrible things. She dreamed about him. The Indian cop. The world was all foggy, and people were screaming all around her, but he was walking toward her, and she was waiting, heedless of whatever danger might be threatening her because he was watching her, coming for her....

She awoke, drenched with sweat, shaking.

She was definitely the wrong woman for this job. She was losing her mind.

No, she had to toughen up. What the hell was wrong with her? She had to be here.

Had to.

Because she, of all people, had to know the truth.

East of the deep swamp, Maria Hernandez plucked the last of her wash from the clothesline. The darkness had come; night dampness had set it. She pressed her clean sheets to her nose, deciding that they still smelled of the sunshine, even if she had cleaned up dinner late and gotten the clothes down even later. Sometimes it seemed that darkness came slowly. Sometimes it descended like a curtain, swift and complete.

But tonight…

Tonight was different.

There were lights. Strange lights appearing erratically down by the canal.

"Hector! Come see!" she called to her husband. He'd been picking all day. He picked their own crops, then rented his labor out like a migrant worker. This was the land of opportunity; and indeed, she had her nice little house, even if it was on the verge of the swamps, but one had to work very hard for opportunity.

"Maria, let me be!" Hector shouted back to her.

"But you must see."

"What is it?"

"Lights."

Hector appeared at the back of the house, a beer in his hand. He was a good man. One beer. Just one beer when he came in at night. He loved his children. They had grown quickly in this land of opportunity, and they had their own homes now. He was a hardworking and very good man. He had provided them with a dream.

But now he was tired.

"Lights?" He had spoken in English. Now he swore in Spanish, waving a hand in the air. "Maria, it's a plane. It's boys out in an airboat. It's poachers. What do I care? Come inside."

But the lights were so strange that Maria found herself walking toward them. The farther she got from the house, the stranger it seemed that there should be lights. What would children be doing out here? Or poachers? Yes, she was on the edge of the swamp, land just grasped from it, but...

Then she heard the noises.

Strange noises...

There was a big lump on the earth. She walked toward it, then paused. Instinctively, she knew she should go back. There were stories about things that needed to be watched out for—things that came from the swamp. Snakes...bad snakes. And there were reports of alligators snatching foolish dogs from the banks of the canal.

She started to back away from the lump on the ground, but then, just as she had instinctively felt that she was facing danger, she suddenly knew that the lump was a dead thing. She kept walking to it.

Clouds drifted against the dark sky, freeing the moon for a brief moment.

It was an alligator, but a dead one.

She didn't know much about alligators. Oh, yes, she lived out here; she had driven along the Trail, seen them basking in the sun. They came in close—the canals were theirs, really, this close to the Glades. But she didn't do foolish things. She didn't try to feed them, heaven forbid! She knew enough to stay away, and little else. But this one was dead, harmless, so she moved closer. And closer.

Because this one seemed very strange.

It had been big, very big. It lay on its back, and it looked almost as if it had been stuffed, and as if all the stuffing had been pulled out of it. There was a strange hole in the center of its chest, as if a fire had burned a perfect circle in the center of the white underbelly. Toes were missing. The jaw gaped open in death.

The lights started flickering again. Maria lifted a hand to her eyes so that they would not blind her.

Her heart quickened.

UFOs! Aliens, spacemen. She was proud of her English; she read all the papers in line at the grocery store. They came down to study earth creatures; they abducted men and women.

She'd seen lights before. Strange lights, late at night. In fact, she'd told her daughter, Julie, about them not so long ago, laughing at her own silliness, because of course Maria had never believed in aliens until now, and Hector scoffed at such silliness. But the lights…

And the alligator…

If they were UFOs, then her initial instinct to run had been right. She had to get back to the house and ask Hector to call the police. Maybe the tall Indian policeman was close by and could help them quickly, far more quickly than the white policemen from the city would make it.

She started to back away. At first it had seemed that the lights were coming from the sky. But now…

They were coming from the brush. From the foliage where the swampland that had not been reclaimed started, just feet from where her lawn began.

Suddenly she was very afraid. She looked at the alligator. A hole in its underbelly. Toes cut off. Eyes…

Eyes cut out.

She turned and started to run.

"Hector!"

A single bullet killed her. A rifle shot straight through her back, tearing through the anterior region of her heart.

Hector heard his wife's scream. He came running out.

The shot that killed him was square between his eyes. He dropped dead still wondering why his wife had called him.

Chapter 2

It had already been one hell of a bad morning.

It had started out with Ginny Hare calling first thing, before it had even begun to be light outside. Jesse was an early riser, but hell, Ginny's hysterical voice before coffee was not a good way to start off the morning.

Billy Ray hadn't come home.

He'd tried to calm Ginny. Lots of times Billy Ray would crash out wherever he'd been and find his way home the next morning.

This was different—Ginny was insistent. He'd gone out fishing with a twelve-pack of beer. And he hadn't come in the morning, the afternoon or the night, and now it was morning again and Billy Ray still wasn't back.

Jesse had tried to soothe her.

"Ginny, I'll get out there looking for him, but you quit worrying. A twelve-pack of beer, Ginny, think about it."

"But, Jesse, he's stayed out two nights!"

"Ginny, I'll look for him, I promise. But he probably got himself as drunk as a skunk and he's sleeping it off somewhere—or, he woke up and knew he'd be in major trouble, and he's trying to figure out how to come home."

When he'd hung up, he'd wondered about the power of love. Billy Ray Hare was the worst loser he'd ever met— white, Indian, Hispanic or black. He hit Ginny all the time, though he denied it, as Ginny did herself. He was her man, and in Ginny's eyes, whatever he did, he was hers, and she was going to stand up for him.

Jesse knew that Billy Ray hated him. That was all right. He had no use whatsoever for Billy Ray. Billy Ray liked to call him "white boy," which was all right, because yes, his father had been white. But his mother could trace her lineage back to Billy, Old King Micanopy, back before the start of the Seminole Wars, back before the government had even recognized the Miccosukee as an independent tribe, speaking a different language from the Seminoles with whom they had intermarried and fought throughout the years. Billy Ray never understood that Jesse was proud of being Indian—and furious when men like Billy Ray fell into stereotypes and became lazy-ass alcoholics.

So Billy Ray was useless. But despite the fact that she loved Billy Ray, there was something very special about Ginny. And for her, Jesse would spend half his day in the sweltering heat of summer looking for her no-good husband.

But he hadn't had a chance to look for Billy Ray yet.

Before he'd gotten out of the house, he'd gotten the call about Hector and Maria Hernandez.

Their property was on the county line, so the Metro Po-

lice were already on the scene. The homicide detective in
charge of the case was Lars Garcia, a man with whom
Jesse had gone to college up at the University of Florida.
His Cuban refugee father had married a Danish model, thus
his ink-dark hair, slim, athletic build and bright powder-
blue eyes. The media liked to make it sound as if the Indian—or Native American cops—were half-wits who were
given only a small measure of authority and who hated
their ever-present big brothers, the Metro cops. Jesse re-
sented the media for that, because it simply wasn't true.
The Metro-Dade force had suffered through some rough
years, with rogue cops and accusations of corruption and
drug abuse. But they'd cleaned house, and they weren't out
to make fools of the Indians policing their own.

Besides which, he'd been a Metro homicide cop himself before making the decision to join the Indian police.

He felt lucky wherever he got to work with Lars when
a body was discovered. Unfortunately, that wasn't a rare
happening.

A swamp was a good place to dump a body. There had
been the bizarre—body pieces dredged up in suitcases—
and there had been the historical: bodies discovered that
had lain in the muck and mud for more than a century.
Man's inhumanity to man was not a new thing. Sad as it
might be, he was accustomed to the cruel and vicious.

Homicides happened.

But the unfairness of homicide happening to good people never ceased to upset him.

Jesse had known Hector and Maria. Known and liked
them. They were as homespun as cotton jeans, without
guile or cunning. She always wanted to bring him in and
feed him; Hector always wanted him to taste a fresh straw-

berry or tomato. They had loved their small home, loved their land more. It was theirs. He'd never seen two people appreciate the simple things in life with such pure and humble gratitude and pleasure.

Uniformed cops were cordoning off the crime scene as he arrived; Lars had been talking with the fingerprint expert but excused himself and walked over to Jesse as soon as he saw him. "Terrible thing, huh? It's technically outside your jurisdiction, but the killers must have come from somewhere. Maybe they were hiding in the swamp, maybe…" His voice trailed off.

"The bodies?" Jesse said.

"You don't have to see them."

"Yeah, I do."

Hector's body was covered when they walked to it; Lars hunkered down and pulled back the blanket. Hector looked oddly at peace. His eyes were closed; he just lay there—normal-looking except for the bullet hole in his forehead. Nothing had been done to the body; the killer probably hadn't even come near him.

"Tracks?" Jesse asked.

Lars shook his head. "None so far. The lawn is all grassy…then there's foliage, and the canal. No tracks yet."

Jimmy Page from the medical examiner's office was still bending over Maria when they reached her. She lay facedown, her head twisted. Her eyes were still open.

She had seen something terrible.

There was a hole through her back.

"Hi, Jesse," Jimmy said, making notes. "I'm sorry as hell, I heard you knew them."

"Yeah. Nice couple. Really good people. Have the children been notified?"

"The son is in the navy, on active duty—they're trying to reach him. The daughter will be here this afternoon."

He winced. Julie was going to come home alone to see her murdered parents. He would have to make a point of being available later.

"Know when she's coming in?"

"American Airlines, two-thirty flight from LaGuardia. Want to meet her with me?" Lars asked.

"Yeah."

"Thanks. I wasn't looking forward to talking to her on my own."

"Have you got anything, Jimmy?" Jesse asked. "I mean…" He looked down into Maria's eyes, thinking he would remember the way she looked for a very long time to come. "This is no drug hit. These people were as clean as they came."

Jimmy shook his head. "Jesse…I've got to admit, about all we're going to know is the caliber of bullet that hit them, maybe the weapon that fired it, an approximate time of death and maybe a trajectory. They were shot," he said, sounding angry. "As to why they were shot…Jesus, you're right. Who can tell?"

"Mind if I take a look around?" Jesse asked Lars.

"Be my guest. We think the killers must have been to the southwest, from the way Maria fell. She was running. Hector was coming to help her."

Jesse nodded, surveying the expanse of lawn. The neat yard the couple had tended so lovingly reached a point where it became long, thick grasses. Back in the grass, the water table began to rise and mangroves grew. Beyond that lay the canal.

He walked carefully to where the thick grass began to

grow, studying the lawn. Although his relations with the Metro police were good, he wondered if any of the beat cops were cracking jokes about an Indian being better at finding footprints than they were.

Hell. He was going to look for them, anyway. He was going to look for anything.

He turned, calling back to Lars, "I think an airboat came through here. See the flattening?"

"Yeah."

"And…" Jesse began, then trailed off. He walked a little further, seeing something in the grass. He moved closer. Bent over. Frowned.

"What is it?" Lars asked.

"Got a glove and an evidence bag?"

"Yeah."

Lars came over to him, slipping his hand into a glove. Jesse pointed to the grass. Lars reached for what appeared to be a branch.

"That?" he inquired. "Jesse, it's just a tree limb."

"No, it isn't."

"Then, what the hell…?"

"It's a gator arm," Jesse said. "From one damn big gator."

"A gator arm? What the hell do I want with a gator arm?"

"I don't know, but where's the rest of the body?"

"It looks like it was sliced off."

"I think the rest of the body was moved, and then this arm tore off."

"But…" Lars began.

"But why? And just where the hell is the rest of the body?"

Lars shook his head. "Maybe…"

"Maybe a dead gator and the murder have nothing to do with each other," Jesse said. "And maybe they do."

"Well, they shouldn't have anything to do with each other," Lars said. "Hell. I can't believe that someone out alligator-poaching would murder two people in cold blood just because he was seen. I mean, it's not as if we execute people for killing gators out of season without a license."

"No, it's not," Jesse agreed. He looked at Lars and shrugged. "But what else is there? Like Jimmy said, there are bullets, there's a time of death…but where the hell is a motive? You're not going to get prints, no fluids for DNA…that's all you've got—an alligator arm."

"I've got nothing," Lars said hollowly.

"Maybe. Maybe not. Send the gator limb to Dr. Thiessen. See what you can get, if anything."

"Of course we'll get it to the vet," Lars said impatiently. "Because you're right. I haven't got anything else. And I'm damned sorry that I may have to tell a young woman who loved her parents that I can't begin to explain why they're dead, except that maybe her mother saw an alligator poacher in the backyard!"

"Lars, you tell me. What else is there?" Jesse said. "This kind of killing looks like an execution, as if it were connected to drugs. But it wasn't. I'd bet my life on that. I'm telling you, Lars, I knew these people. They were bone clean."

"They must have seen something, then. They must have known something, but…you're sure? I mean, sometimes we think we know people, but they're living double lives."

"No. I knew them, Lars."

"All right. Maybe the daughter can help us."

"I doubt it. But I'll go with you. I'll talk to her with you. But, Lars, after today…you'll keep me informed on this one all the way, right?"

"Yes."

"No matter what goes on in Homicide?"

"Yes!"

"Swear it?"

Lars looked at him, arching a brow. "We're already blood brothers," he reminded him with a rueful grimace.

Jesse stared at him, shaking his head. Yeah. Forever ago, when they had been young and going to college.

Strangely, or so it seemed now, their college mascot had been an alligator.

They had both pledged the same fraternity. It had been during that period that they'd been out drinking together and Lars had gotten into the blood brother thing, having seen one too many John Wayne movies, Jesse decided.

"Yeah, blood brothers," Jesse returned, surprised that he could almost smile, even if that smile was grim.

"Jesse, the only thing—"

"I won't go off half cocked to shoot to kill if I find out who did it. I'm a cop. I'll bring them in."

Lars watched him for a moment. Jesse locked his jaw, staring back at his friend. Maybe Lars had the right to doubt him. When Connie had died…

Fate had kept him from killing the man who had murdered her. But there had been no question in his mind that, given the chance, he might well have committed murder himself in turn, so great had been his rage.

"I'm telling you, I'll be a by-the-book lawman." He shook his head, sobering. "They didn't deserve this, Lars."

"I swear, I will keep you up on what's happening. I'll have to—the killer or killers probably came from the swamp and maybe ran back that way. We'll have lots of our guys in your territory."

"I'll brief my men, as well."

"Get a warning out to them right away."

"Will do."

"You want to take this piece of gator over to Doc Thiessen?" Lars asked him. "You're more familiar with the damn things than I am." He didn't add, Jesse noticed, that he was probably also far more convinced than Lars was that the alligator remains might have something to do with the case.

They started back toward the house. Jesse found himself pausing by Maria's body. The forensic photographers were still at work. He looked into her eyes. In Metro Homicide, he'd seen a lot. A bullet was a fairly quick, clean way to die. He'd seen mutilations that had turned even his strong stomach.

But this...

He'd seen her face alight and beautiful when she'd smiled.

"Jesse, quit looking at her," Lars said.

"Yeah. Well, I'll inform the office, then get out there looking for Billy Ray Hare."

"Billy Ray? You don't think—"

"That Billy Ray killed these two? Not on your life. Billy Ray may be a drunk, and he may not be a prime husband, but he keeps to himself and wouldn't step outside the area he's accustomed to. And he'd also be too damned drunk to make it this far by that time of night. I've got work to do, and so do you. I'll meet you at two so we can get to the airport. Where?"

"The restaurant at the turnpike entrance."

"I'll be there," Jesse said.

When he left, his first stop was the vet's. Dr. Thorne Thiessen was a rare man, pleased to live deep in the Everglades, and fascinated more by birds and reptiles than the more cuddly creatures customarily kept as pets. He was such an expert with snakes that people traveled down from Palm Beach County, a good hour or so away, to bring him their pythons and boas, king snakes, rat snakes and more.

He was in his early fifties, both blond and bronzed, almost as weathered as some of the creatures he tended with such keen interest. He was just finishing with a little boy and his turtle when Jesse arrived, bearing the alligator limb.

He looked at Jesse with surprise. "People usually call on me with living creatures, you know."

"Yeah, but Metro-Dade and I both think you can help on this one. You *are* the reptile expert. You can make some preliminary findings, then pass some samples upstate. Hopefully, someone will figure something out."

Thiessen had been smiling; now he frowned. "What have you got?"

"What do you think?"

"I think it's a piece of an alligator."

"Great."

"No, no, I can do tissue and blood samples, do a profile…and get samples upstate, just like you suggested, but why?"

Jesse explained. Thiessen stared at him for long moments. "And you found this at the scene?"

"Yes."

"Jesse…"

Jesse sighed. "They weren't into drugs."

"Still, they might have witnessed an exchange in the Everglades, or, hell, God forbid, another murder."

"They might have. But this is what we've got for now."

Thiessen shrugged. "Big sucker," he said.

"Yep," Jesse agreed.

"I'll do what I can," Thiessen promised.

Jesse thanked him. In the waiting room, he looked for Jim Hidalgo, who worked for the vet, but then he remembered that Jim worked nights.

The man at the desk was a big guy, John Smith. He was so big, in fact, that he was almost apelike. Jesse didn't remember when he hadn't been with the vet.

Good man to have on, Jesse thought. Big enough to cope with any animal out there.

At least, almost any animal out there.

He grunted to Jesse in a combination of hello and goodbye.

Come to think of it, a grunt was the only conversation Jesse had ever shared with the man.

He waved and went out.

"Look into the eyes of death! Stare into the burning pits of monster hell. See what it would have been like to face the hunger and rage of a carnivore older than the mighty *Tyrannosaurus rex!* Ah, but, believe it or not, once upon a Triassic age, this was an even more ferocious and terrifying creature, in fact, one that made minced meat of the mighty dinosaurs themselves." Michael Preston paused for effect as he talked to the small, wriggling creature he held in his right hand.

The week-old hatchling let out a strange little squeaking sound, its jaws opening, then snapping shut. The eyes were yellow with central stripes of black. It was small, almost cute in a weird sort of way, but the mouth shut with a pressure that was chilling, despite its size.

The hatchling began squealing and wriggling again.

"Loudmouth," Michael said, shrugging. He liked the fact that the American alligator made noise. Noise was good. Noise was warning. "But you *are* being awfully dramatic here," he told the hatchling. "Okay, so I'm a little dramatic myself. Because I *hate* tour groups," he grumbled.

Even as he slipped the hatchling back into its tank, the door to his lab opened and Lorena entered.

"Watch out—the monsters are coming," she warned.

Michael arched a brow. "Monsters," she whispered, emphasizing the warning. Then she turned, a beautiful smile plastered on her face as she allowed room for the tour group to enter. Ten in all, a full tour: two young couples, perhaps on their way to register for college, maybe on honeymoon. They looked like ecology-minded types, surveying the wonder of the Everglades. There was an attractive, elderly woman, probably a widow, seeing the Sunshine State now that old Harvey or whoever had finally bitten the dust. Then there was a harried-looking couple with three boys who looked to be about twelve. The woman had once been pretty. The man had a good smile and looked like a decent father. The boys seemed to be the monsters. They walked right up to his lab table, barged against it, then leaned on it, peering into his tanks and petri dishes.

"Uh, uh, uh—back now," Michael said, frowning at Lorena as if she might have forgotten to warn her group that the tour was hands-off. She shrugged innocently and grinned back with a combination of mischief and amusement. No doubt the boys had been a handful since they'd started their tour. Actually, Lorena wasn't responsible for leading tours. She was a trouper, though. She seemed to like to be in the middle of things; when there were no injuries or sniffles to attend to, her work was probably boring. And it wasn't as if there were a dozen malls or movie theaters in the area to keep her busy.

"Back, boys," he repeated. "Even hatchlings can be dangerous."

"Those little things? What can they do?" demanded the biggest boy as he stuck his hand into the tank with the week-old hatchlings.

Michael grabbed his hand with a no-nonsense grip that seemed to surprise the boy.

"They can bite," Michael said firmly.

"Mark Henson, stand back and behave, now," the boy's obviously stressed mother said, stepping forward to set a hand on Mark's shoulders. "We're guests here. The doctor has asked you—"

"He ain't no doctor—are you?" the boy demanded.

The woman shot Michael an apologetic look. "I'm so sorry. Mark is my son Ben's cousin, and I don't think he gets out very often."

"It's all right," Michael said. He was lying. Mark was a brat. "Mark seems to be very curious. Yes, Mark, I *am* a doctor. I have a doctorate in marine science. Salt- and freshwater reptiles are my specialty. I also studied biochemistry, animal behavior and psychology, so trust me, hatchlings can give you a nasty bite. Especially these hatchlings."

"Why *those* hatchlings?" Mark demanded immediately.

Because we breed them especially to chew up nasty little rugrats like you! he was tempted to say. But Lorena was already answering for him.

"Because they're tough little critters, survivors," Lorena said flatly. "Ladies and gentlemen, Dr. Preston is in charge of our selective-breeding department. He knows a tremendous amount about crocodilians, past and present. He'll tell you all about his work now—for those interested in hearing," she finished with just the slightest edge of warning in her voice for the boys. They stared at her as she spoke, surveying her intently. No wonder she was glad to let the group heckle *him* now. Lorena was an exceptionally attractive woman with lush hair, brilliant eyes, and a build that not even a lab coat could hide.

The two older boys were at that age when they were just going into adolescence, a state when squeaky sopranos erupted every ten minutes, and sexual fantasies began. And they were obviously having a few of those over Lorena. She made a face at Michael surprised him by slipping quickly from his lab. Well, she didn't have to be here, he told himself. It wasn't her job. But she'd seemed fascinated by everything here ever since she'd arrived.

Even him.

Not that he minded.

Except that…

She was bright. And really beautiful. So what was she doing out here?

She was good with people, he would definitely give her that. The complete opposite of the way he felt. He hated having to deal with people.

He gave the boys a sudden, ever-so-slightly malicious smile. "Well, gentlemen, let me introduce you more fully to these hatchlings. Alligators, as you might have heard already, date back to prehistoric times. They didn't descend from the dinosaurs. They were actually cousins to them. They shared common ancestors known as thecodonts. And way back in the late Cretaceous period, there was a creature called Deinosuchus—a distant relative of these guys—

with a head that was six feet in length. Imagine that fellow opening his jaws on you. True crocodilians have been around for about two million years. They're fantastic survivors. They have no natural enemies—"

"That's not true!" Mark announced. "I saw a program on alligators and crocs. An anaconda can eat an alligator, I saw it. You could see the shape of the alligator in the snake. Man, it was cool—"

"We don't have anacondas in the Everglades," Michael said, gritting his teeth hard before he could continue. "Birds, snakes and small mammals eat alligator eggs, and it's easy for hatchlings to be picked off, but once it's reached a certain size, an alligator really only has one enemy here. And that's…?"

He let the question trail off, arching a brow toward Mark. He looked like a jock. Probably played football or basketball, at the very least. He liked to talk, but he didn't seem to have the answer to this one.

"Man," said one of the boys. He was thinner than his companion, with enormous dark eyes and long hair that fell over his forehead. Nice-looking kid. Shy, maybe, more of a bookish type than Mark. "Man is the only enemy of a grown alligator in the Everglades."

"That's right," Michael said, an honest smile curving his lips. He could tell that this kid had a real interest in learning. "You're Ben?" Michael asked.

The boy nodded. He pulled the third kid up beside him. "This is my other cousin, Josh."

"Josh, Ben and Mark."

"Do we get to see the alligators eat a deer or something?" Mark asked.

"Sorry, you don't get to see them eat any living creatures here, kid. The juveniles and adults out in the pools and pens are fed chicken."

"They're so cool," Ben said, his brown eyes wide on Michael.

Michael nodded. "Yep, they're incredible. Alligators were near extinction here when I was young, but then they became protected. The alligator has made one of the most incredible comebacks in the world, mainly because of farms like this, but also in the wild. They look ugly, and they certainly can be fearsome creatures, but they have their place in the scheme of life, as well, keeping down the populations of other animals, often weeding out the sick and injured because they're easy prey."

"I think they're horrible creatures," Ben's mother said with a shudder.

"Some people hate spiders—but spiders keep down insect populations. And lots of people hate snakes, but snakes are largely responsible for controlling rodent populations," Michael said.

"What's that mean?" Mark asked.

"It means we'd be overrun by rats if it weren't for snakes," Ben answered, then flushed, staring at Michael.

"That's exactly what it means," Michael said.

"What do you do here, Dr. Preston?" the third kid, cousin Josh, asked.

"That's easy. He's a baby doctor for the alligators," Mark insisted.

"I study the growth patterns of alligators," Michael said. "We raise alligators here, but this is far from a petting zoo. We farm alligators just like some people farm beef cattle. We bring tourists in—and other scientists, by the way, to learn from the work we do here—but the owners are in this for the same reason other farmers work with animals. For the money. Alligators are valuable for their skins, and, more and more, for their meat."

"Tastes like chicken," Mark said.

"That's what some people say," Michael agreed, bristling inside at the boy's know-it-all attitude. "They're a good food source. The meat is nutritious, and little of the animal goes to waste. We're always working on methods to make the skin more resilient, the meat tastier and even more nutritious. By selective breeding and using of the scientific method, we can create skins that improve upon what nature made nearly perfect to begin with."

"Perfect?" Ben's mother said with a shudder. Her husband slipped an arm around her.

"They make great boots," he said cheerfully.

"Belts, purses and other stuff, too," Ben supplied.

"You'll see more of that as your tour progresses," Michael said. "I'll tell you a bit more about what goes on in here, then you can watch them eat, Mark, and at the end, guess what?"

"We can all buy boots, belts and purses made out of alligator skin?" one of the young women inquired with a pleasant smile.

"That's right," Michael agreed.

"And we really get to see them chomp on chickens?" Mark demanded, as if that were the only possible reason for coming on the tour.

"Yeah, you can see them chomp on chickens," Michael agreed. He pointed at Ben. "Come back here, Ben, and you can help me." Michael looked up at the adults in the crowd. He never brought a kid back behind his workstation, but for some reason, it seemed important to let Ben lord it over

Mark. He was sure that life usually went the other way around. "One of the most incredible things we're able to do in working with crocodilians is studying the growth of the embryo in the egg. Ben, lift that tray, so they can see what I mean."

"Wow!" Mark gasped, stepping forward again. Even he was impressed.

"It's possible to crack and remove the top of the alligators' eggs to study the growth of the embryos without killing them. It's also possible to cause changes and mutations in the growing embryos by introducing different drugs, genetic materials or even stimuli such as heat or cold. Here…in this egg, you'll see a naturally occurring mutation. This creature cannot survive even if it does reach the stage of hatching. You see, it's missing a lower jaw. Can you imagine an alligator incapable of using its jaws? Everywhere in nature, there are mishaps and imperfections. Over here, in this egg, you have an albino alligator. They have tremendous difficulty surviving because—"

"Because they sunburn!" Mark interrupted, laughing as if he'd made a joke.

"Actually, that's true. They have trouble coping with the intense sun that their relatives need to survive. They also lack the element of surprise in their attacks—they're easily seen in greenish or muddy waters where their relatives are camouflaged by their surroundings."

"He's a goner," Mark said.

"Well, not here," Michael told him. "He'll hatch and grow, and he'll have a nice home at the farm, and we'll feed him and take care of him—you know why?"

"Why?"

"Because he's unusual, and our visitors will like looking

at him, that's why," Michael said, pleased with himself because he seemed to be growing a little more tolerant of Mark.

"So that's what you do—you try to make white alligators?" Mark asked.

Michael shook his head. "Selective breeding…well, it's
what makes collies furry or Siamese cats Siamese. We find
the alligators with the best skins and we breed them, and
then we breed their offspring until we create a line of animals with incredibly hardy skins that make the very best
boots and bags and purses. We also find the alligators that
give the most meat with the most nutritional value—"

"Because it's a farm, and it's out to make money," Ben's
mother said, and she shuddered again. "Thank God!"

"She thinks you should kill them all," Ben's father said.

Michael shrugged. "Like I said—"

"They should all be killed," the attractive older woman
said, speaking out at last. She had keen blue eyes, and she
stared at Michael, somehow giving him the creeps. "They
eat people."

"They *do* eat people, right?" Mark demanded with a
morbid determination.

"There have been instances, yes."

"A friend of mine was eaten!" the elderly woman said,
and she kept staring at Michael, as if it was all his fault.

"Anytime man cohabits with nature, there can be a certain danger," he said gently. He looked at the others. "It's
dangerous to feed alligators. The alligators are repopulat-
ing Florida, and they do get into residential canals, especially during mating season. I know of one incident in
particular when a woman was feeding the alligators…and,
well, to the alligator, there is no distinction between food
and a hand offering food."

"And children," the woman said, growing shrill. "Children! It's happened. It's horrible, and they should all be destroyed. Little children, just walking by lakes, looking at flowers—these monsters need to be killed! All of them! How can you people do this, how can you!" Her voice had risen; she was shouting.

There was a buzzer beneath his workstation; all Michael had to do was hit it and the security people would come. Sign of the times—you never knew what kind of dangerous lunatic might walk in with a tour group. But Michael didn't touch the button; the older woman had stunned him by suddenly going so ballistic, and he just stared at her.

She pointed a finger at him. "Tell them. Tell them the truth. Tell them about the attacks."

"Yes, there have been attacks, and of course that's horrible. But we need to live sensibly with nature. In Africa, along the river, the Nile crocodiles are far more ferocious, but they're a part of the environment. We can't just eliminate animal populations because the animals are predators. We're predators ourselves, ma'am."

She shook her finger at him, and her voice grew more strident. "They're going to eat you. They're going to eat you all. Rise up and tear you to pieces, rip you to shreds—that's how they do it, you know, little boy!" she said, suddenly gripping Mark by the shoulders. She stared at him with her wild eyes. "They clamp down on your body, and they shake you, and they break you and rip you, and your bones crunch and your veins burst. Your blood streams into the water, and you're dying already while they drown you."

"Oh, my God, please!" Ben's mother cried, trying to pull Mark from the woman's grip.

"Hey now!" Michael said, and he came around his station, setting an arm around the woman's shoulders to hold her while Ben's mother, pale as a shadow, pulled Mark to her.

"You!" the elderly woman said, turning on him again. "You! They'll eat *you*. You made them, and they'll eat you. They'll tear you to bits, and your own mother won't be able to find enough bloody pieces to bury you!"

"Now, really, I didn't invent alligators, ma'am—"

"You'll die!" she screeched.

He reached for her again, aware that he had to take control of the situation before it became a monumental disaster. He could see her going completely insane and destroying his lab. Then the cops would be called in, and soon reporters would be crawling everywhere, and then…

"Please, now—" he began.

The door suddenly opened. Security hadn't come; Lorena had, presumably drawn by the noise. She stared reproachfully at Michael.

"What happened?"

"That lady is telling Dr. Preston that the alligators should eat him!" Mark said excitedly.

"We have a problem," Michael agreed. "I think I should call Security—" he began.

"No, no, we're all right." Lorena—who, he had been told, had a degree in psychology and another in public relations, as well as being an RN—assessed the situation quickly and took charge. "Mrs. Manning, right? Come along and tell me about it. We'll get you something cold to drink. It can be so hot here, even with the air-conditioning on the heat can get to you and—"

"Young woman, I am not suffering from the heat!" the elderly woman proclaimed. But her shoulders sank, and she suddenly seemed to deflate. "I'm sorry, I'm sorry. I'm not a lunatic, I don't usually behave this way.... I shouldn't have come. Yes, young woman, you may get me something cold to drink."

Lorena led her quickly toward the door, but once there, the woman stopped and turned back, staring at Michael. She pointed at him again. "I hope they don't eat you, young man," she said. Then she smiled, but it wasn't a pleasant expression, and despite himself, he felt the strangest chill snake along his spine.

Then she was gone, as Lorena whisked her out the door.

Michael, with the nine remaining members of the tour group, was dead silent as seconds ticked by.

He suddenly felt a small hand slipping into his. He looked down. Ben was staring up at him. "Don't worry. She was just crazy. She probably had a friend who got eaten, and she probably misses her. I'm sure you're not going to get eaten, Dr. Preston."

Michael smiled; the chill dissipated.

"All right, everyone. I have a question for you. What animal is most dangerous to Americans?"

There was silence for a moment, then Mark cried out, "I know, I know! Bees!"

"Bees are up there in the top ten, but they're not in the number-one slot."

"I know what it is." A young man, one of the two who looked like a newlywed, was speaking for the first time. He held his wife tightly against him, and seemed pale himself, probably shaken by the older woman's display. "The deer."

"The deer?" Ben protested.

"That's right," Michael said.

"The deer? You mean like *Bambi?*" Josh asked.

"More Americans are killed each year due to accidents involving deer than are killed by any rattler, spider, shark or reptile out there. So we have to remember to always be careful in any animal's environment," Michael said.

His door opened again; Peggy Martin, one of the guides, stepped in. "Well, ladies and gentlemen, it's time to move on to the pens, or straight into either the gift or coffee shop, if you'd rather," she said cheerfully.

"Mark, you get to see the gators eat chickens," Josh said.

Mark looked at Ben's parents. "I'm really hungry. Maybe we could just get a hamburger. Please?" he said politely.

"Sure, sure," Ben's father said. He looked at Michael. "Thank you for the information, Dr. Preston."

"Yeah, it was great," one of the pretty young women Michael had pegged as a newlywed agreed.

"Thanks," Michael said. "Thanks very much, you were, er, a great group."

He leaned back against his workstation, strangely exhausted. The old woman had given him the creeps. He kept a false smile plastered to his face as the group filed out, the boys in the rear.

Mark was the last. Before he exited, he turned back, looking uneasy.

"Dr. Preston?"

"Yes?"

The boy seemed about to say something, but then he shook his head. "Thanks. You were all right."

Michael nodded.

"Come back sometime," he told Mark, wondering if he meant it or not.

"Yeah."

The door closed behind Mark.

The hatchlings began to squeak.

Chapter 3

In the gift shop, Josh began to play with a two-foot-long plastic alligator. "I've got five dollars," he told Ben. "Think this looks real?"

"Yeah, it's cool," Ben told him.

Mark walked up to the pair in the corner of the shop. He still looked a little pale—they had all been kind of spooked, the old lady had been *really, really* creepy, scarier than the alligators—but he was kind of swaggering again, which Ben was sure meant that Mark was all right.

"That don't look real, Josh. Not compared to this!"

Reaching into the pocket of his baggy, oversize jeans, he pulled out one of the hatchlings. The little creature's mouth was opened wide. Tiny teeth were already chillingly visible.

"Mark! You stole one of the hatchlings—" Josh began.

"Shh," Mark protested.

"Oh, man, you've got to give that back," Ben said.

"No way," Mark said. "Look at him!"

The jaw opened, snapped.

Mark shoved the hatchling toward Josh, who jumped back. "Don't do that, Mark."

"He's going to eat you all up," Mark said, laughing as he started to stuff the creature back into his pocket.

But suddenly he cried out, his hand still in his pocket.

"Oh, shut up," Ben commanded. His cousin was big stuff around school; he had looked up to Mark, and he'd wanted to be like him. But Ben had never been on an outing like this with Mark before. Mark was always on, like maybe there were always girls watching or something. Now the way people were staring was just embarrassing. "Come on, Mark, stop it. People are looking—"

Mark jerked his hand from his pocket. "Get it off! Get it off!" he screamed. The hatchling had his forefinger in its mouth. To Ben's amazement, there was a trail of blood dripping down his cousin's finger.

Instinctively, he reached for the hatchling. But Mark started screaming again. "No, no, don't pull. You'll tear my whole finger off!"

People were beginning to stare. Ben pushed Mark toward a rear door. It read No Admittance: Staff Only, but Ben ignored that; the way the buildings were set up, he could tell that the door led back into the hallway where the labs were housed.

"What are we doing? Where are we going?" Mark cried frantically. "Oh, my God, it hurts! He's eating me!"

"Shut up, shut up, we're taking him back!" Ben said. He moved Mark faster and faster down the hall, pushing back into Dr. Preston's lab without knocking at the door.

Dr. Preston was there, thankfully, standing almost where they had left him. He started when they entered, standing taller in his lab coat. He wasn't very old for a doctor; he was tall and nice-looking, with sandy hair and green eyes, and if Mark hadn't been such a jerk—and if the old lady hadn't freaked out—he might have spent more time with them and told them a lot more neat stuff.

"What the—" Dr. Preston began.

"Mark took one of the babies, but it bit him and we can't get it off and we're real sorry, honest to God, we're real sorry, but can you help—"

Preston helped. Right away, he knew where to pinch the hatchling so that it let go rather than ripping. He dropped the hatchling back into a tank. By then there were tears in Mark's eyes, ready to spill down his face.

"Come over here," Preston said to Mark, taking him back behind his workstation, washing the wound at a sterile-looking sink, then covering it with some slimy cream. "We'll have to take you to the nurse and tell your folks—"

"No, please, no!" Mark protested. "I'm here with Ben's parents. If my parents ever found out I—that I tried to steal from this place, they'd…"

Preston stared at Mark, then at Ben, and then at Josh, who had followed them, silent and so white that his freckles stood out on his face.

"Mark, you were bitten—"

"It's a tiny hole. Look, you can barely see it."

"Yes, but—"

"I've had a tetanus shot, honest."

"Mark, there's always a rare chance that reptiles can carry disease—"

"Not alligator-farm reptiles!" Mark said. "Please, please, please don't say anything. You don't know my dad."

Preston hesitated.

"Please," Mark whispered. "Please,"

Ben held his breath. Preston was staring at Mark, studying his face.

The door behind them quietly opened and closed. Ben jumped, turning around. It was their first guide, the really pretty lady with the dark hair and bright blue eyes.

She didn't say anything, just leaned against the door, watching the situation. Dr. Preston looked at her. He lifted Mark's fingers. "They were trying to leave with a souvenir."

"Ah…" she murmured to the boys. "What were you going to do? Drop him in your hotel swimming pool?" She turned to Dr. Preston. "I need to look at that, and then we need to file a report."

Mark went pale.

"I was thinking about letting him go. I think he already paid enough of a price," Dr. Preston said.

Ben was surprised to see that the beautiful nurse was the one who seemed to think they needed the authorities. She was staring at Dr. Preston. "We really shouldn't take the chance. Just in case there are consequences, an infection…"

Dr. Preston stared back at her. "This is one of the cleanest labs you're ever going to find." He sounded indignant.

The nurse, however, wasn't backing down. "I don't know…."

"Please," Mark begged.

"Hey, I'd never let anything happen to a kid," Dr. Preston swore. "Though this one…all right. Call in the authorities."

"No, please," Mark begged.

The woman stared at Dr. Preston for a moment longer.

Then she looked at the boys. They were staring at her with downright prayers glittering in their eyes.

She nodded, a smile twitching at her lips; then she walked over to look at Mark's finger. Her glance at Michael assured him that it was a minor injury. "We have some antibacterial medicine to put on that."

Preston stared at Mark. "You know, Ms. Fortier has a point. This is against my better judgment. I could lose my job. I could be sued. Who knows, maybe I could go to jail. Lorena, could I go to jail for this?"

"I don't know, but there's a cop outside. Jesse Crane." She made a tsking sound. "I've heard that he feels passionately about people messing with things like this. The Everglades, well, this place is his passion. So I've heard."

"I'll never say a word, never, even if my finger drops off—even if my whole hand explodes!" Mark swore.

Lorena pulled a tube of cream from her pocket and dabbed some of the contents on the injured finger.

She took a bandage from another pocket and covered the bite. When she was finished, though, she was in a real hurry. "I've got to get back to the office. I just came by to make sure everyone was okay. That poor woman is still…well, in bad shape."

"This is just a tiny bite," Mark said apologetically. He gulped. "Thank you, Nurse," he murmured.

She took off. Preston watched her go.

Ben was surprised and pleased to see that Dr. Preston was actually smiling when he said, "Mark, you take this as a lesson. And if your hand swells up, don't keep it a secret. Tell the doctor you stuck your hand in the tank and got bitten by a hatchling, and then you have them call me right away, got it?"

"Yes, sir," Mark swore.

He turned, flying for the door. Ben ran after him. At the door, Mark stopped. Ben crashed into him. Josh, always close, crashed into Ben.

Mark didn't notice the pileup. He was staring back at Dr. Preston. "Thanks, Doc. Honest. I'll make it up to you one day."

Preston nodded at him.

"Okay. I'll hold you to your word."

The boys hurried back out to the gift shop. Ben plowed right into his mother.

"There you are! Thank God. If you're buying anything, do it now. I can't wait to leave this place. Honestly, Howard," she said to his father, "couldn't we have taken them on an overnighter to Disney World? I can't believe we're going from here to an airboat ride and a night in one of those open-air chickee things!"

"It will be fine, dear," Ben's father said. He winked at Ben.

"I knew I should have gone with Sally and the Girl Scouts," she said.

Ben flashed a quick smile to Mark. Mark smiled back. It was going to be all right.

No one was in trouble. The alligator farm wasn't going to call the police or Mark's parents; Ben's folks weren't even any the wiser.

The day was saved.

The airboat ride was next.

Jesse had pulled into the parking lot at the alligator farm already tired. He hadn't found Billy Ray, though he'd found Billy Ray's boat. Where the hell the man had crawled off to, he didn't know. He would need lots more time to comb the swamp to find Billy Ray.

Just what he needed to be doing when two friends had been shot down in their own yard for no apparent reason.

And now this.

A call because a woman had gone into a fit while visiting the alligator farm.

Lots of tourists, he noticed. That was good. Along the Tamiami Trail, a lot of the Miccosukee Indians depended on the tourist trade for a living. Along Alligator Alley, stretching from Broward westward across the state in a slightly more northerly route, a lot of the state's Seminole families depended on the tourist trade, as well. The big alligator farms pulled people in, and then they stayed and paid good tourist dollars for airboat rides, canoe treks along the endless canals at sunset, and even camping in traditional chickees. The locals made money, which was good, because they needed it.

Of course, the biggest earner in the area was the casino. Still, there were a lot of other good ways to make a living from tourists. Either way, it was money honestly earned, and to Jesse, the setting alone was worth the price of admission. The Everglades was a unique environment, and though civilization was steadily encroaching on the rare, semitropical wilderness, it was still just that: a wilderness. Deep in the "river of grass," a man could be so entirely alone with God and nature that civilization itself might not exist. There were miles and miles, acres and acres, where no one had as yet managed to lay a single cable or wire; there were places where even cell phones were no use. There were dangerous snakes and at times the insects were thick in the air. But it was also a place of peace unlike anything else he'd ever experienced. Every once in a while he thought of himself as a rare individual indeed—a man finally at peace with himself, satisfied with his job, and certain, most of the time, that he was the best man for it.

At least, he usually felt at peace with himself and as if he could make a difference in his work.

Today…

Today the world didn't make sense. That a couple as fine and hardworking as Maria and her husband could meet such a fate…hell, what good were the police then? Even if they solved the crime, his friends were still dead.

But thanks to his work, he wasn't powerless. He would find the killers and see justice done. That was his job, and it was one worth doing.

He wasn't making a fortune or knocking the world dead, but he didn't need money. He needed solitude, and the opportunity to be alone when he chose. And he needed to feel that he had some control over his own life and destiny, and this job certainly gave him that. Sometimes, he was very much alone, but that was a choice he had made, consciously or perhaps subconsciously, when he had lost Connie.

"Jesse!"

Harry Rogers, major stockholder and acting president and supervisor of Harry's Alligator Farm and Museum, hurried toward Jesse, who got out of his car. Harry was a big man, six foot two by what sometimes appeared to be six foot two of girth. He often talked like a Cracker, having been born in a Deep South section of northern Florida, and he was proud of being a Cracker, even if he'd gone on to acquire a degree in business administration from none other than such a prestigious Yankee institution as Harvard.

"Thank God!" Harry exclaimed, clapping him on the back. "We got a lady went berserk in the middle of Michael's speech, started screaming that he was going to get eaten up, and going on and on about how dangerous the gators were. I didn't want the Metro cops coming in here with their sirens blazing and all…and God knows, we don't need the community up in arms about the gators any worse than they already are, but…"

"Where is she?"

"My office, and is she a loose cannon or what? I'm telling you, she's downright scary. I've got Lorena, the new nurse, with her. We made her some tea, Lorena's talking to her, but she's still going off every few minutes or so."

Harry stopped talking and looked at Jesse closely. "Hey, what's the matter? You look grim."

"I am. An old Cuban couple in that new development east of here was murdered."

"How?"

"Shot."

"That your jurisdiction?" Harry asked, scratching his head.

"No, but they were friends."

"I'm sorry. Real sorry. Were they into drugs?"

That was the usual question, especially in a shooting. "No, it had nothing to do with drugs."

"You sure?" Harry asked skeptically.

Jesse gritted his teeth. "Yes, I'm sure."

"Well, if I can help…but at the moment, you've got to be a cop here for me, since this is your jurisdiction."

"All right. I'll see what I can do, but if this lady has really lost her mind, we may need some professionals out here, and we may have to call in the county boys."

"I hate the county boys."

"Hell, I like to settle our own problems, too, Harry. You know that."

"Sure do," Harry said. "'Course, you're the only man among us I've seen put those boys down."

"There are good county cops, Harry. We're a small community out here."

"We're an Indian community," Harry said dryly.

"Doesn't matter. We're small. You have to have the big boys around when you need real help. Hopefully, we don't need it now. Do you know where this woman is from? Has she said?"

Harry shook his head. "Every time we ask her, she goes on about her friend who was eaten. She's got to live near a lake somewhere, but that could be half the state. Don't that just beat all? The old broad has a friend eaten by a gator—so she comes to visit a gator farm. Folks are weird as hell, huh?"

"Folks are weird," Jesse agreed without elaborating. The whole thing was weird, he thought. The woman here had a friend who'd been eaten by an alligator.

A piece of an alligator had been found where two innocent people had been murdered.

He followed Harry in through a side entrance to the administrative buildings and down a long hallway.

The place might be an alligator farm out in the swamp, but Harry knew how to furnish an office. It was at the end of a long hallway. A single door opened onto a room with a massive oak desk surrounded by the best in leather sofas and chairs. To the rear were more seats, a large-screen TV-and-VCR combo, and floor-to-ceiling speakers for his elaborate sound system. Harry loved the Everglades; he even loved reptiles. He was part Creek, not Seminole or

Miccosoukee, but he'd worked his way up from cotton picking at the age of three to millionaire businessman, and he liked his creature comforts. His office might have been on Park Avenue.

Jesse could hear the woman as he followed Harry in. She was speaking in a shrill voice, talking about how nothing had been found of "Matty" other than a hand with a little flesh left on the fingers. Jesse glanced at Harry, then walked over to the woman, who was standing in a corner, flattened against the wall. Her hair was silver, her eyes a soft powder blue. She was trim and very attractive, except that now the flesh around her eyes was puffy from crying, and she gazed around with a hunted, trapped look of panic on her face.

In front of her, trying to calm her, was a young woman in a nurse's standard white uniform. Jesse couldn't see her face because a fall of sleek, honey-colored hair hid her features, but before she turned, he knew that he'd already met her.

And she was certainly the last person he'd expected to see at Harry's.

A woman who looked like that and drove a car like that, pedal to the metal…

To get *here?*

She stared back at him for a fleeting moment, instantly hostile—or defensive?

"You're going to get eaten!" the woman was shrieking, pointing at the nurse. "You've got to get out of here. Don't help these people breed monsters. They'll kill you, too. Crush you, drown you… Oh my God, a hand, a hand was all that was left…some flesh, just bits and pieces of flesh…."

"Hey, now, ma'am," Jesse said, stepping forward, trying to remember what he had learned in Psychology 101. "It's going to be all right, honest. Calm down. The alligators here are being raised as food. They're no danger to anyone on the outside—"

"They'll get loose!" the woman protested. But she had given Jesse her attention. He had kept his voice low, deep and calm—Psychology 101—and his firm tone seemed to be working with her. He stepped closer to her, reaching out a hand.

"They're not going to get loose. No one's going to let them get loose." He smiled. "Besides, Harry here is a charter member of the National Rifle Association. He and his staff wouldn't hesitate to shoot any gator that moved in the wrong direction. He's not out to save the gators, ma'am, he's out to make money off them."

She took his hand, staring into his eyes.

Next to him, Jesse heard a deep sigh of relief. He glanced at the woman standing by him, Harry's new nurse. Despite himself, he felt a little electric tremor.

Nature, simple biology, kicking in.

She was probably one of the most beautiful women he had ever seen.

Harry had a habit of finding pretty girls. Strange that a fat old man who owned an alligator farm could convince any young woman to come work in the middle of a swamp. Not that Harry was a lecher; he was as faithful as could be to Mathilda, his equally round and cheerful wife of thirty-odd years. But he did like attractive young people, and he had managed to fill the place with them, so this new nurse shouldn't have been too much of a surprise. Still, Jesse felt himself pause, as he hadn't in a very long time, staring at her.

Maybe it was just the day he'd had so far.

She looked back at him gravely, studying him with the same intensity as he had studied her. Then she looked down, biting her lower lip, embarrassed. In a moment she looked up again, straightening her shoulders and inclining her head, an acknowledgment that he had defused an uncomfortable situation. Her eyes were a dark-rimmed light hazel, startling against the classical, pure cream perfection of her face. Her hair was like a halo of crowning glory; she looked almost fragile in her blond beauty, yet he sensed that there was a lot of substance to her, as well.

He felt the warmth of the older woman's hand and, with a start, looked back to the gray-haired visitor—his current objective. He gave himself a little shake, surprised that Harry's new nurse had so impressed him, and continued to talk to the older woman. "It's okay. We're going to get you home. Except you're going to have to give us a bit of a hand to do that," he continued. "I'm Jesse Crane, a police officer out here. I'd like—"

"Oh!" the woman cried. "So now you're going to arrest me for telling the truth about these monsters and the horrible people purposely breeding them."

"No, ma'am, I just want to get you home and make sure you're going to be all right."

"Oh, like hell. You're just trying to shut me up!"

Jesse smiled at her. He couldn't help it. She was a tough old broad. She might be going over the edge, but she was going with passion and style.

"What's your name?"

"Theresa Manning."

"How do you do, Mrs. Manning? You're free to call the newspapers, or buy a banner ad and have a plane drag it through the sky. We guarantee freedom of speech in this country. But you're hot and miserable, and if you lost a friend to an alligator, this is not a good place for you to be. Let me take you home."

Theresa Manning hesitated, then sighed deeply.

"Where is your home?" he prodded.

"The Redlands."

"All right." He glanced at his watch. It was important to him that he meet Lars to go to the airport and pick up Julie Hernandez. "Let's go. Let me take you home now."

She nodded, looking at him. But as she rose, she suddenly gripped the nurse's hand.

"You, too. Please."

"But, Mrs. Manning—" the nurse protested.

"Please," Theresa Manning insisted.

"Go with her," Harry said softly to the nurse.

"Harry, I won't be able to bring her back for a while," Jesse said.

"Oh, please," Theresa Manning said, starting to grow hysterical again.

"Lorena, just go with him. When you get back, you get back!" Harry said impatiently.

Lorena's startling eyes fixed on Jesse's, and she said, "All right. If Mrs. Manning wants me with her, I'll be with her, and whatever you have to do, Officer, I'll wait until you're able to get me back. Shall we go?"

Jesse lifted his hands in surrender. He almost smiled. Maybe she felt this was her way of getting back at him for what had happened yesterday.

Fine. If she wanted to wind up involved in a murder investigation and not get back until the wee hours of the morning, so be it.

"Yeah. Sure. Let's go," he said flatly. "Mrs. Manning?" He smiled, taking the older woman's arm. She actually smiled back.

He let Lorena follow behind as he escorted Theresa Manning from the office to his car.

Damn, this was one hell of a day.

Chapter 4

Lorena sat in the back of the car, while Theresa Manning sat in the front with Jesse Crane.

She felt somewhat useless being there, but the woman had been insistent. And though Lorena felt a twinge of guilt, aware that she had been eager to come not so much to help out—which she certainly was willing to do—but because she wanted the time with Jesse Crane.

As Sally had pointed out, the man was something special. But that wasn't why she was interested in him.

Despite the heavy traffic, he drove smoothly and adeptly. They left the Trail and headed south. He kept up a casual stream of conversation with Mrs. Manning, pointing out birds, asking about her home and family. By the time they neared her neighborhood, she seemed relaxed, even apologetic. Jesse told her not to be sorry, then suggested that she not take any more tours in the Everglades for a while.

At her house, she asked them in. Jesse very respectfully declined, but he gave her a card, telling her to call him if she needed him.

When they got back in the car, Lorena told him, "That was impressive."

He shrugged. "The woman isn't a maniac, just really upset. And maybe feeling that kind of rage we all do when something horrible has happened and we're powerless to change it." He glanced at his watch, then at her. "Sorry, I have to get to the airport, and it's not going to be pleasant."

"I told you...whatever you need to do...do it. I'll hang in the background," Lorena said.

He nodded, and after a few minutes she realized that he was heading for the turnpike. He glanced over at her, a curious smile tugging at his lips. "What brought you to our neck of the woods?" he asked her.

She shrugged, looking out the window. Then she looked at him sharply. "Well, I thought you'd already figured that out. I was racing out to one of the resorts. A spa. To be pampered."

"I'm sure you'll find time to slip out and hit some of the prime places," he said dryly.

"Really?" she murmured.

He couldn't resist a taunting smile. "You do your own hair and nails?" he asked.

"As a matter of fact, I do," she told him.

He shook his head. "You don't look the type," he said.

"You have to look a type to work out here?"

"You'll burn like a tomato in a matter of minutes," he warned her.

"They do make sunscreen," she returned.

"So...I repeat, what are you doing out here?"

"The job at Harry's," she said simply.

"There are nursing jobs all over the state. And most of them not in the Everglades."

She gazed over at him, surprised to realize that she was telling the truth when she said, "I like it out here."

"You're fond of mosquitoes the size of hippos and reptiles that grunt through the night?"

"I think the sunsets out here are some of the most beautiful I've ever seen. As to the alligators…well, they're just part of the environment, really. The birds are glorious. And the pay's exceptional."

"I see. Well, it's still a lonely existence."

It was her turn to smile. "Okay, so it may take an hour to get anywhere, but…it's a straight shot east to Miami and a straight shot west to Naples. Not so bad."

"I guess not. But in bad weather, you can be stuck out here and feel as if you're living in the Twilight Zone."

"You came back out here to work," she said softly.

There was silence for a minute. "This is home for me," he said.

"It's not so far off from home for me," she said.

"It's pretty far."

She glanced at him sharply.

"Jacksonville. I took your license, remember? And now that I know you were flying like a bat out of hell to reach Harry's, I'm more stunned than ever."

"I was starting a new job," she said defensively. "And however far it might be, I *am* from this state." Great. Now he was curious. What if *he* decided to investigate *her?*

She noticed that they had left the turnpike and were following the signs for the airport. He glanced at her again. "I'm meeting with a Metro-Dade detective. We're meeting a detective named Lars Garcia and picking up an old friend of mine." He hesitated just slightly. "That's why I didn't want you along. It's not going to be pleasant. Julie's parents were murdered last night."

"Oh, my God! I'm so sorry."

"I warned you."

"What happened?"

"They were shot," he said flatly.

She decided not to ask any questions for the next few minutes. He'd obviously been deeply affected by the murders.

They parked at the airport. Jesse knew where he was going and walked quickly. Lorena followed him. Outside Concourse C, he walked over to a man in a plain suit, a man with light brown hair and green eyes, but dark brows and lashes. Even before she was introduced, Lorena knew that this was Lars Garcia.

She felt the keen assessment he gave her. Part of his job, she imagined. Summing people up quickly.

"So you're working out at Harry's?" he murmured.

She didn't have time to answer.

"There she is," Jesse said softly, spotting his old friend, Julie.

"I'll go," Lars Garcia offered.

But Jesse shook his head.

He left Lars and Lorena, and walked toward the dark-haired, exotic-looking Latin beauty who was coming their way. She was wearing glasses, apparently to hide the redness in her eyes, which was apparent when she saw Jesse and took them off. Then she dropped the overnight bag she'd been carrying and went into his arms, sobbing.

Lorena looked down, feeling like an intruder. "It's all right," Lars Garcia said softly.

She looked up at him.

"They're just good friends."

Lorena felt her cheeks flush hotly. "No, no, don't get the wrong impression. I'm just here…by accident, really. I barely know Officer Crane."

Lars Garcia continued to assess her as Jesse, an arm around Julie, led her to where Lorena and Lars stood waiting.

"Julie, this is Detective Lars Garcia. He's in charge of the case," Jesse said. "And this is…Lorena. Lars, Lorena, Julie Hernandez."

Julie offered Lorena a teary, distraught but somehow still warm smile.

"Julie, I'm so sorry," Lorena murmured, feeling totally inadequate and wrenched by the girl's pain. She could all too easily remember the feelings of agony, frustration and fury, and always the question of why?

And after that, the *who?*

And now?

And now the gut-deep fury and determination that the truth would be known.

"Thank you." Julie looked at her for a long moment, as if sensing Lorena's sincerity. Then she turned to Garcia. "Whoever did this…why? My parents never hurt a soul in their entire lives."

"We're going to find out why," Lars vowed softly. "We need your help, though. We need anything you can give us."

Julie visibly toughened then, summoning her anger and determination from deep within, her inner reserves rising over the natural agony she was feeling. "I was just telling Jesse… I have no idea. They had no enemies. But I promise you, I'll help you in any way I can."

"Are you up to coming to the station with me now?" Lars asked. "It can wait, if you'd rather."

"No. No, I'll go now," Julie said, and swallowed. She looked at Jesse. "Jesse…?"

"Call me when you're done."

She nodded, trying to smile.

Lars took Julie's arm and cast a grateful glance over her dark head at Jesse.

The two walked off.

"I'm so sorry," Lorena said. She had never met the couple, but the sense of loss had seemed to envelop her. Impossible to see Julie and not feel it. She felt horrible, like an intruder, again. "I…wish there were something I could say, do."

Jesse nodded, then said only, "I can get you back now."

The silence, growing awkward between them, lasted as they left the airport, taking the expressway to the Trail, then heading straight down the road that stretched the width of the southern tip of the peninsula.

They passed homes and developments, and then the casino. After that, houses and businesses became few and far between.

She was startled when Jesse suddenly said, "Can you give me another half hour?" He turned and looked at her with those startling eyes of his. She wondered if he had decided he didn't feel quite so much contempt for her, or if he was merely so distracted he'd barely even been aware till then that she was there with him.

"I…of course. Of course. Harry said it was no problem," she murmured.

They pulled off onto something she wasn't sure she would have categorized as a road. As they proceeded along a winding trail, she realized that they were on farmland.

A minute later, she saw the crime tape. Jesse Crane pulled off the road.

"Excuse me. Stay here—I'll be just a minute," he said.

He exited the car, leaving her in the passenger's seat. Lorena hesitated for the briefest fraction of a second, then followed him.

She wasn't about to stay.

Jesse wasn't in the area enclosed by the tape. He was standing just outside of it, talking to a uniformed officer and a man in street clothes who had an ease in being there that suggested he was also a cop.

As she walked up, she could hear the man in street clothes talking. "Yeah, Doc Thiessen has the gator arm... the leg, whatever, that you discovered. I really don't see how it's going to help us. The Hernandezes were killed by bullets, not wildlife run amok!" He saw Lorena approaching before Jesse did, and he watched her, curiously and appreciatively, as she walked up to the scene.

Jesse turned to look at her with annoyance, a serious frown furrowing his brow.

"I told you to wait in the car," he said coldly.

"Hello, ma'am," the young uniformed officer said.

"Yes, hello," the man in plainclothes said. "How do you do? I'm Abe Hershall."

"Officer Gene Valley, ma'am," the uniform said.

"How do you do?" She shook hands with the tall, slender, dark-eyed man who was obviously a detective, and the uniformed officer. Jesse stood by silently, waiting, not apologizing for his rudeness, and certainly not offering any information about her.

"I'm working at Harry's," she said herself.

"The new nurse," Gene Valley said. "Well, welcome to the area."

"Thanks," she said softly.

"Working for old Harry, huh?" Abe Hershall said, shaking his head ruefully. "Well, good for Harry."

"This is a crime scene," Jesse reminded them all. "Ms. Fortier, now that you've met everyone, I believe it's time for me to get you back."

Taking Lorena by an elbow, he steered her forcefully back to the car.

"I can walk on my own," she said.

"I told you to stay in the car."

"It's a million degrees in there." She looked him in the eye. "Who was that?" she asked. "Abe…is he Lars's partner?"

"Yes."

He forced her determinedly back into the car. The door slammed. She gritted her teeth.

"You found a piece of a gator out there?" she asked when he was in the driver's seat.

"This is the Everglades. There are lots of alligators, and naturally, some die." He put the car in gear and started driving, his eyes straight ahead.

"But you found a *piece* of one."

Jesse slammed on the brakes, turned and stared at her, angry. Whether with her, or with himself, she wasn't sure. "Look, we found a piece of an alligator, yes. And I'd appreciate it if you would just shut up about it. I'm trying to keep that bit of information out of the press. You see, I'd really like to know if there's a connection between that and a murder. Damn! This is all my fault. I shouldn't have brought you out here, and I sure as hell shouldn't have counted on you staying in the car just because *I told you to!*"

Lorena looked straight ahead. "I have no intention of leaking any information," she said.

He stared at her. "Really? And should I ask for that as a guarantee, written in stone? After all, I don't know anything about you."

She grated her teeth. "Do I look like someone who would shoot an innocent couple?"

"No. But you don't look like someone who'd be working at Harry's, either," he said sharply.

She let out an explosion of exasperation. "I don't suppose you'd believe I actually like it out here?"

"Right. Nothing like being a nurse at an alligator farm," he murmured.

"Maybe it's just an easy gig," she said.

He didn't reply. Her heart sank. She had a feeling that he was going to know everything there was to know about her within the next forty-eight hours.

Maybe she should just tell him.

Maybe not. He obviously thought of her as some kind of fragile cream puff. Maybe a rich brat playing games. She shouldn't have brought her own car, she thought, hindsight bringing sudden brilliance.

If he found out anything about what she was doing, he might well find a way to get her out of Harry's—fast. Even that evening.

Could he do such a thing? Was he good friends with Harry—or whoever was involved?

She kept silent.

A few minutes later, they drove back into the complex that comprised Harry's Alligator Farm and Museum.

"Thanks," Lorena murmured, getting ready to hop out of the car as quickly as possible.

He caught her hand lightly. She held still, not meeting his eyes, but careful not to make any attempt to jerk free. She realized that he frightened her. Not because she thought he would hurt her, but because he aroused something in her, something emotional. She found herself waiting to tell him everything, wanting just to be with him.

"Be careful," he warned softly.

"Of…?" she murmured.

"Well, an elderly couple was just shot," he said impatiently.

"I'll be all right," she said. Then she pulled free. There was something far too unnerving about his touch. She didn't like the fact that though she barely knew him, she respected him already. Admired him. Even *liked* him. "Thanks."

"I'll be seeing you," he said pleasantly.

"Of course," she said, and then, at last, she managed to flee.

There wasn't much daylight left, but since Ginny had called in to the station several times saying that Billy Ray hadn't yet come home, Jesse decided it was time to check out his fishing spots.

Billy Ray was lazy, a creature of habit, and Jesse wasn't surprised when he found the man's beat-up old boat at his first stop in the vast grounds off the Trail.

The boat had been floating in the middle of the canal—already suspicious—and there was no sign of Billy Ray.

Jesse began walking along the embankment. At first he let his mind wander, mentally reminding himself that he had a record of Lorena Fortier's driver's license, enough to find out something about the woman. Frankly, he admitted to himself, he was worried about her. He could hardly say that he knew her from their two encounters, but there was something about her eyes, about the very real compassion she had shown the elderly woman, that made him feel she was—despite his original assessment—a decent human being.

There was something about her that made him feel a lot more, as well. Now that he'd gotten closer to her, it was far more than the simple fact that she was stunning, though that was good for a swift, hot rise of the libido. She was quick to show empathy, and in the right way. She seemed to sense pain and use her warmth to heal it. Her energy was electric.

Sensual.

He swore out loud, reminding himself that he was here trying to determine what had happened to Billy Ray Hare.

Still…

She had roused not just his senses, but thoughts that he had kept at bay for a long time. There was nothing casual about her. She evoked real interest—and very real desire. But, he realized, not the kind that could be easily sated, then forgotten.

What was it about her?

Her eyes? Her behavior? Or the way she looked? Like a blond goddess, tempting in the extreme.

He mentally shook his head, reminding himself again that this wasn't the time to discover that there was life not just in his limbs, but in his soul. Two good people had been murdered, and Billy Ray was missing. This definitely wasn't the time to be feeling a stab of desire just because a woman had walked into his neck of the woods.

Still, even as he concentrated his attention on the wet

ground, the endless saw grass and the canal, he felt a strange sense of tension regarding *her.*

She was involved. Somehow, she was involved.

Just as that thought came to his mind, he found Billy Ray. What was left of him.

Sally finished up with the day's entrance receipts, locked her strongbox and papers in the safe, and smoothed back her hair. Quite a day. All the commotion.

So much going on. Admittedly, most of the time so little went on here. That was why she had to make things happen. With that in mind, she started humming.

She was done for the day.

She walked determinedly down the hallway. News, any little bit of it, spread like wildfire around here. She loved to be the first to know any little tidbit.

She headed across the center of the complex.

"Hey, Sally!"

She smiled at the man leaning against one of the support poles.

"Hey, yourself," she said softly. Teasingly. It got boring out here, after all.

"Got anything for me?" he asked softly, since there were still both tourists and co-workers around.

She walked up to him, smiled, placed a hand lightly on his chest. "Maybe," she murmured seductively.

"Maybe?"

"Well, it depends."

"On what?"

"On what *you've* got for *me,*" she whispered.

She let her hand linger for a moment. A promise, just like her whisper. Then she walked away.

She could be warm; she could give.

But she fully intended to receive in return. After all, there was pleasure.

And then there was business.

The gates had closed; the last of the tourists were flooding out as Lorena returned. She headed straight for her room, a quick shower and a change of clothes.

Though she wasn't accustomed to choosing her wardrobe for the purpose of seduction, she did so that night. A soft, pale blue halter dress seemed the right thing—cool enough for the summer heat, a garment that molded over the human form. She brushed her hair until it shone, then played with different ways to part it. She found a few of the effects amusing, but decided to go back to a simple side part and a sleek look. A touch of makeup, and she was off.

She found Dr. Michael Preston in the company cafeteria. The kitchen was centrally located between the employee dining area/lounge and the massive buffet area where visitors were welcome. During the day, a head chef worked with two assistants and three buffet hostesses. By night, only the offerings of the day and two cafeteria workers remained.

Alligator—sautéed, fried and even barbecued—was always on the menu. Lorena had dined on it in the past, but tonight she didn't want it, not in any form.

As she'd expected, she saw Michael Preston—who hadn't ordered gator, either—sitting with the keepers, the blond Australian, Hugh Humphrey, and the tall, striking Seminole, Jack Pine.

The three men rose as she approached. Jack whistled softly. "Wow! And welcome. Are you joining us?"

"If you don't mind."

"Are you kidding?" Hugh demanded pleasantly.

"You're definitely a breath of beautiful fresh air around this place," Jack assured her.

"Please," Michael Preston said, pulling out a chair.

She smiled, thanked him and sat down.

"I heard we had a bit of a freak-out today, and that you went with Jesse to take the woman home," Jack said. "Bizarre, huh?"

"Her friend was…eaten," Lorena said softly. "Why she was out here after that, I don't know."

Michael made an impatient sound. "Do you know what happens most of the time when gators kill? Some idiot thinks you can feed them like you feed the ducks at a pond." He shook his head. "First we destroy their natural habitat. Every year, development spreads farther west, into the Everglades. Naturally there are waterways. Then people wonder what the alligators are doing in their canals."

"Well, trust me," Jack said ruefully, his tone light and teasing, "you're not going to stop progress."

Hugh looked at Lorena seriously. "You're not afraid of being eaten, are you?"

She shook her head. "Trust me, I have no intention of feeding the gators. I'll leave that to you guys."

"Man is not the alligator's natural prey," Michael said. "Go out to Shark Valley. You can walk those trails, and, trust me, there are hundreds of gators around, but they don't bother anyone."

"It really is unusual, and there's always a reason, when a human is attacked," Jack explained. "Most of the time Hugh and I get called because a gator has strayed into a heavily populated area. We catch it and bring it back out to the wilds. The end."

"Do you ever keep the ones you 'rescue'?" Lorena asked.

"No. We breed our own alligators here," Michael said. "Harry's been here a long time now. He started up with a small place when they were still really endangered, so a couple were captured. But now all our gators are farm raised, because they do make good eating. And their hides make spectacular leather. Farms like this one are an important part of the state's economy. They're much more than just tourist attractions."

Lorena smiled. "They really are fascinating creatures," she told Michael. "I'm absolutely intrigued by your work."

"Cool," Jack said, folding his arms over his chest and leaning back. "We get a nurse who not only patches up our scrapes, she's into the entire operation. I hear that you don't mind working with the tour groups, either."

She shrugged. "I'd die of boredom here if I weren't interested."

"Hey, did you want something to eat?" Jack asked her.

She turned slightly to see that one of the remaining kitchen workers was standing by her side.

"Mary, have you met Lorena yet?" Jack continued, speaking to the heavyset woman at his side.

Mary shook her head, then pointed across the room to where Harry was sitting, engaged in conversation with Sally.

"The boss said to check on you," Mary said, looking at Lorena. "Usually people come up to the buffet. So are you hungry? You'd better eat now. We break down in half an hour, then there's nothing except the vending machines until morning—unless you want to drive for an hour to find something open." She shrugged. "You go into Miami, you got some places open twenty-four hours a day. But you want to drive back here in the middle of the night?" Mary shuddered. She'd been looking grim, but then she smiled. "You want some alligator?"

"Um, actually, no, thank you," Lorena said. "Is there another choice?"

"There's always chicken," Michael offered, grinning at last.

"How about a salad?" Lorena asked. She wasn't a vegetarian; she just didn't think that at the moment she wanted meat of any sort. Especially crocodilian.

"Caesar?" Mary suggested.

"Lovely."

"Of course, we do offer the caesar with a choice of chicken, sirloin or alligator," Mary said.

"A plain caesar would be perfect," Lorena said.

Mary shrugged, as if a plain caesar was probably the least appetizing thing in the world. "Something to drink?"

Lorena ordered iced tea and thanked Mary, assuring her that she would know to go to the buffet herself from then on.

When Mary was gone, Jack Pine nudged Lorena, his dark eyes dancing with amusement. "She's all right, really. Just a bit grim."

"She doesn't like alligators at all," Michael said.

"Why does she work out here?" Lorena asked.

"Harry pays well," Michael said. He leaned forward suddenly. "The guys and I were going to head to the casino for a few hours. Want to come?"

"We'd love to have you," Jack said.

"You look far too lovely to hang around here," Hugh said, grinning.

If they were all leaving, this might well be her best

chance to get into Michael's laboratory. She yawned. "Actually, I'd love to take you guys up on that, but at a later date? I'm just getting accustomed to my new surroundings, and I'm feeling pretty tired."

"You really should come," Michael said, placing a hand over hers.

She smiled at him, as if enjoying the contact. "I will. Next time," she said sweetly.

Mary arrived with her salad. The men remained politely waiting for her to eat, then rose together when she was done. Lorena said that she would walk them out to the parking lot, then head for her room.

The three men climbed into Jack Pine's Range Rover, and she waved.

As soon as they were gone, she headed for the inner workings of the museum.

And Dr. Michael Preston's lab.

Lars and Abe stood by Jesse on the embankment, watching as the M.E. bagged the remnants of Billy Ray.

At the moment, Jesse felt the weight of the world on his shoulders.

There was no one else who could go to see Ginny. This was going to be his responsibility, and with the Metro-Dade force on the scene, that meant he could go to her now.

But he hesitated, seeing the floodlights illuminate the immediate darkness and feeling the oppressive heat of the ebony beyond.

"I don't believe it," Lars said, staring in the direction of the M.E., shaking his head.

"I'm not quite sure I do, either," Jesse said. He pointed. "The best I can figure it, Billy Ray was in his boat. His shotgun was still in it, and it had been fired. It looks as if an alligator actually rammed the boat, Billy fell out, and… well, you know how they kill, shaking their prey, then drowning it."

"Alligators don't ram boats," Lars said.

"Looks like this one did," Jesse said.

Abe frowned, staring at Jesse. "Alligators may follow a boat, looking for a hand out—literally." He smiled grimly. "But they don't ram boats. I'd say maybe someone was out here with Billy Ray. Maybe they fought. Maybe Billy Ray even shot at him. Then the fight sent him overboard, and a hungry old male might have been around. A really hungry old male, since we all know gators don't choose humans."

"Gentlemen, this is my neck of the woods, and God knows, I want tourists out here as much as anyone, but I'd say it was time we get some kind of warning out," Jesse said.

"Warning?" Abe protested. "Like what? Don't head into the Everglades? Killer alligators on the loose?"

"Yeah, something like that," Jesse said flatly.

Abe shook his head. "Jesse, you're nuts. What do you want to do, destroy the entire economy out here?"

"I'll tell you this, I intend to issue a warning," Jesse said.

"Hey, you do what you want," Abe said.

"What the hell are you saying?" Jesse demanded, his temper rising. "We all know that Billy Ray was killed by a gator."

"How do we know that?" Abe demanded. "Seriously. You do an autopsy I don't know about?"

Jesse stared at him, incredulous. "What?"

"We have a ripped-up body. You said yourself that Billy Ray's gun had been shot. Maybe someone shot back at him, he wound up in the water, bleeding, and then the gator attacked him. That's a far more likely scenario."

"Stop it," Lars protested. "Both of you. We've got a bad situation here."

"Yeah, we do. A couple shot to death—with the remains of an alligator found nearby. Now a fellow who knew this place better than any living human being, killed by an alligator. If that isn't enough—" Jesse said.

"That couple were killed because they saw something going on in the swamp—I'd lay odds on it. And alligators don't shoot people," Lars argued. "These incidents are totally unrelated."

Jesse just stared at him, so irritated he longed to take a jab at Abe's out-thrust, obstinate jaw. Instead, he turned and walked away. "You do what you want. So will I."

"Hey!" Lars called after him.

Jesse turned back.

"Jesse…you may want to be on the lookout for a…well, I don't know. A rogue alligator. A big one," Lars suggested.

"Yeah. Are you going to contact the rangers, or should I?" Jesse asked.

"I'll see that they're notified," Lars assured him grimly.

Abe snorted. "Yeah. We'll handle this one by the book. This is your neck of the woods, Jesse. Billy Ray was one of yours. Homicide only comes in when we've got a murder. We'll see that the site is investigated, and then we'll sign off on it. This is your ball game."

"And I'll get warnings out on Indian land. And I also intend to arrange a hunt."

"It ain't season, Jesse," Abe said.

Jesse crossed his arms over his chest. "Maybe not, but it *is* tribal land. Like you said, it's my call. At the least, we're talking about a nuisance animal. I'll be taking steps."

Abe threw up his hands.

"This one is your call, Jesse," Lars told him.

"Fine. And you know the call I've made. You put out the warnings in your territory."

"Because of one alligator?"

"How do we know it's just one?" Jesse demanded.

"And how do we know Billy Ray didn't just drink himself silly, then irritate the creature—a normal, everyday predator that happens to live out here—and make the mistake of going in right where a big boy was hungry?"

"What was an alligator limb doing out where Hector and Maria were killed?" Jesse demanded.

Abe shook his head. "People murdered with big guns—and a natural predator attack. There's no damned connection!"

"Hey," Lars said. "The matter will be under investigation."

"Abe, I'm warning you, there could be a lot more trouble," Jesse said.

"Great. I'm warned," Abe said.

"Jesse, no one is going at this with a closed mind," Lars assured him. "Hell, I'm a cop, not a kindergarten teacher. We're professionals. We'll complete our investigation of the scene and sign this one over to you. Abe, dammit—you know as well as I do that anything is possible. All right, children?"

"Sure," Abe said.

"Yeah," Jesse said. "You're right. And now I have to go talk to a woman about the fact that her husband is dead."

Abe snorted. "She should be relieved."

Lars exploded, swearing.

Jesse turned away.

He couldn't put it off any longer. He had to go to see Ginny.

And then…
Then he would have to talk to Julie.
The night ahead seemed bleak indeed.

Chapter 5

Since she was carrying a lock pick in her purse, Lorena had no problem waving with a smile as the car drove away, then heading straight back inside and down the hall to Dr. Michael Preston's lab.

She stood for several seconds in the hallway, but the place was entirely empty.

There were guards on duty, of course. But they were outside, protecting the alligator farm. She had made a point in the beginning of seeing whether there were cameras in the hallways, but there weren't—not unless they were exceptionally well hidden.

She headed for the door, reaching into her purse.

"Lorena!"

Stunned, she spun around. Michael was there in the hallway, right behind her.

"Hey!" she said cheerfully, approaching him quickly.

"I thought you were going to get some rest tonight?" he said, frowning.

"I changed my mind. I was hoping to find you."

"In the hallway? You just waved goodbye to us."

"I don't know—sixth sense, maybe. You're back, and I'm so glad. I can still go with you. If you're still going."

He nodded. "I forgot my cell phone, so I came back to get it."

"Great. I'll wait for you."

He nodded, still appearing puzzled, but she kept her smile in place, following him into the lab.

The hatchlings squeaked from their terrariums.

Lorena stood politely by the door, waiting. As she had before, she inventoried what she could see of the lab.

The file cabinets. Michael's desk. The pharmaceutical shelves. The computer.

He took his cell phone from the desktop, then joined her. She linked arms with him, and felt the tension in him ease.

"Are you a poker player?" he asked her.

"Not really," she admitted.

"There's not too much else," he warned.

"I love slot machines," she assured him.

He smiled back at her. Apparently her attempt at flirtation was working. He slipped an arm around her shoulders. He was a good-looking man, with a sense of humor, and though it seemed he sometimes wondered if he were too much of an egghead in comparison with the rugged handlers, he apparently also had faith in his own charisma. "Let's head out, then, shall we?" he asked, and there was a husky note in his voice. If she was happy in his company, it apparently wasn't too big a surprise to him.

Then again, she'd been trying to keep the right balance. Flirt just the right amount with the bunch of them.

"Let's head out," she agreed, and she fell into step with him, aware of his arm around her shoulder—and also aware that the lab was where she really needed to be.

Jesse had a feeling that Ms. Lorena Fortier from Jacksonville would be quite surprised when she learned that the Miccosukee police department currently consisted of a staff of twenty-seven, nine of them civilian employees, the other eighteen officers deployed throughout the community in three main areas: north of the Everglades in Broward County; the Krome Avenue area, encompassing the casino and environs; and the largest center of tribal operations, on the Tamiami Trail. The pay was good, and the Miccosukee cops were a respected group. The department had been created in '76, because most of the tribal areas were so remote that a specific force was necessary to protect the community, and to work with both the state and federal agencies in tracking down crime.

The force had four specialized units: Patrol Services, the Bureau of Professional Standards, the Background Investigations Unit and the Records Section. Jesse wondered if Lorena was under the impression that he was working as the Lone Ranger.

Before he made his dreaded trip to Ginny's place, he returned to the station. His crews were up on everything that happened in the jurisdiction, but he hadn't been back in himself yet, and he disliked being in a situation where communication wasn't tight as a drum.

The night crew was coming on, but he was in time to catch the nine-to-fivers and give everyone his personal briefing on both the double homicide and the death of Billy Ray.

He liked being at the office; he wasn't a one-man show, but the department was still small enough that every officer and civilian employee knew that they mattered, and that their opinions were respected. He got the different departments researching activities in the area, possible drug connections, the backgrounds of Hector and Maria, and anything that might strike their minds as unusual, or any kind of connection.

Barry Silverstein, one of the night patrolmen, was especially interested in the alligator limb that had been brought to the veterinarian for examination. "Strange that you found only a piece," he said. "Think maybe we're looking for a poacher?" he asked.

"Could be," Jesse said. "But it's not likely. We have an alligator season, and a license is easy enough to obtain. Besides, the alligator farms have pretty much taken the profit out of poaching."

"Kids?" Brenda Hardy, the one woman on night duty, inquired. "You know, teenagers, maybe. Or college students. Say that the piece of the alligator has nothing to do with the murders. Maybe some kids pledging a fraternity or just making ridiculous dares to one another."

"I sure hope it's not a trend," Barry said. "They may have gotten that gator, but you start playing around with some of the big boys out there…well, hell, we know what they're capable of."

"Poor Billy Ray," Brenda said sadly, shaking her head. She was a pretty woman, tall and slim, and all business. She was light-skinned and light-haired, probably of Germanic or Nordic descent. You didn't have to be Native

American to be on the force. Barry, who was Jewish and had had ancestors in the States so long he didn't know where they'd originally come from, always liked to tease her that she was an Indian wannabe. Brenda had once gravely shut him up by assuring him that she had been a Native American in her previous life.

"I'll tell you frankly that this situation scares the hell out of me. These people are brutal and ruthless. Everyone has to be alert," Jesse warned.

George Osceola, one of the native officers on the force, a tall man with huge shoulders and a calm, controlled way of speaking that made him even more imposing, had been watching the entire time. He spoke then. "Jesse, you think these incidents are related, don't you. How?"

"That's what I can't figure. Murders that cold-blooded are usually drug related. And we're not ruling that out," Jesse said.

"Could we be dealing with some kind of cult?" George asked.

"I don't know. What I do believe is that we've got to get to the bottom of it fast. George, ask questions, see if anyone has seen anything out of the ordinary. People coming through who aren't out to enjoy nature or a day at the village. Strangers who hang around. Anything out of the ordinary. *Anything.* Metro-Dade homicide is working the murders. I'm afraid we may find the killers closer to home."

"We'll all be on it," Brenda said.

Jesse nodded. "Brenda, do me a favor. Get background investigations busy for me, will you?"

"On the Hernandez family?" Brenda asked, sounding puzzled.

"No. On a woman named Lorena Fortier. I just wrote her a ticket, so we'll have her driver's license information. Find out more about where she comes from, what she's been doing."

"Lorena Fortier?"

"She just started working at Harry's."

"All right," Brenda said, still puzzled, but asking no more questions.

"You going out to Ginny's now?" Barry asked.

"Yeah," Jesse said. "And then to see Julie."

No one replied. No one offered to take on the responsibility. He didn't want them to, and they knew it. These were things he had to do.

He left to see Ginny, and it was rough. As rough as he had expected.

Eventually he left Ginny with her sister and niece, both of whom apparently thought that Billy Ray had come by accident to an end that he deserved. Thankfully, they weren't saying that to Ginny, though; they were just holding her and soothing her. Anne, Ginny's niece, had told him that as soon as possible, she was going to take her aunt away for a while. For the moment, they had called the doctor, who had prescribed a sedative for her.

Before he left, Ginny had gripped his hand. Her large dark eyes had touched his.

"Help me, Jesse—please. Find out…find out what happened."

"Ginny, he met with a mean gator," her sister said.

But Ginny shook her head. "Billy Ray knew gators. Jesse, you have to help. I have to know…*why.* Oh, God, oh, God…Jesse I need to know, and you're the only one who can help."

With her words ringing in his ears, he had gone on to meet Julie.

Hell of a night.

So now he sat with his old friend in the upstairs bar of the casino hotel where she had chosen to stay. Julie had told him that she appreciated his offer to let her stay at his place, but she had wanted to be closer to the city and couldn't quite bring herself to stay in her parents' house.

He agreed that she shouldn't stay at her folks' house— certainly not alone. Neither he nor the Metro-Dade police had any idea what had happened, and the houses in that area were way too few and far between for him to feel safe with her there.

"I'm telling you, Jesse, there's no way my folks were connected to anything criminal," Julie said, at a loss. "I'd give my eyeteeth to help. In fact…I think I could kill with my own bare hands, if I knew who did this. But they were as honest as the day is long."

"I know that, Julie."

She sighed, running a finger around the glass of wine she had ordered. "I'm glad you're on this, Jesse. The other guys…they didn't know my folks."

"Lars is a good man. So is Abe. A bit of an ass, but a good detective."

That brought a hint of a smile to her lips. "Still, no matter what you tell people… Everybody seems certain that my dad had turned a blind eye to some drug deal, at the very least. The thing is, you and I both know that there was no such thing going on."

"Of course." He patted her hand. "Did your mom or dad ever say anything to you about anything strange going on out there?"

Julie shook her head. "No." She hesitated, frowning. "Actually, once…" She fell silent, shrugging.

"Once what?"

"Oh, something silly. It can't have anything to do with what happened," Julie said.

Jesse touched her hand. "Julie, I don't care how silly you may think something sounds. Tell me what it is."

"Um, well, I lose track of time, but a few days ago, maybe a week, when I was talking to my mom, she was getting into talking about ETs. You know, extraterrestrials."

"Oh?"

"She said there were weird lights. I'm sure it was just someone out in an airboat, but…"

"But?"

"Well, my mom was getting on in years, but her vision was good. She thought the lights were coming from the sky. That's why she got it into her head that aliens were searching the Everglades."

"A lot of planes come in that way," Jesse pointed out.

"The lights from planes don't stay still."

"Helicopters," Jesse said.

Julie shrugged. Then her face crumpled and she began to cry. Jesse didn't try to tell her that it would be okay. He just came around the table and held her.

Helicopters. If anything big had been going on—the police searching for someone, for instance—he would have known about it.

Maria had had fine eyesight, no more fanciful than the next person. And she had seen lights.

Jesse knew that there had been an airboat behind the house the night Julie's parents had been killed. That wasn't surprising. Airboats abounded. But helicopters…

They were uncommon, especially in that area. Not unless someone was looking for something.

But in the middle of the night?

"Jesse, what could it have been?" Julie whispered, as if she had been reading his thoughts.

"I don't know. But I swear, Julie, I will find out."

The casino didn't compare with a place in Las Vegas or Atlantic City—there were no roulette tables and no craps—but it was nice, and it was apparently quite convenient for people in Miami with a free night but not the time to really get away.

It was thriving when they arrived.

The three men tried to encourage Lorena to try her hand at one of the poker tables, but she managed to convince them that she preferred slots and would be happy wandering around, just getting to know the place. There were several restaurants, and though there were tables offering free coffee, she opted for café con leche at the twenty-four-hour deli. She noted the numerous security officers and stopped to chat with one young man. His name was Bob Walker, and he had bright blue eyes, thanks to a dad who had come to the States from the Canary Islands, and superb bone structure, thanks to a Seminole mom. He told her that Casino security departments and the Miccosukee Police were two separate entities, but of course they worked together, just as Security would work with the Metro-Dade police or any other law enforcement agency. He'd sounded a little touchy at first, but as they spoke, he explained with a grin, "Too many gamblers drink, lose and get belligerent. And they think we can't take care of them. We do. We have the authority."

She grinned. "I don't intend to get rowdy," she assured him.

He flushed, and she thanked him and went on.

The place was big, and she wandered a while before finding a slot machine that looked like fun. It had a little mouse, and a round where you got points for picking the right cheese. She liked the game—it might be stealing her money, but it was entertaining.

Out twenty bucks, she left to walk around some more.

It was fascinating, she thought. The crowd was truly representative of the area, running the entire ethnic gamut. Miccosukee, Hispanic, Afro-American, and whatever the blend was that ended up as Caucasian on a census form.

She could see the poker tables and was aware that, from their separate poker games, the guys were also keeping an eye on her.

She was frustrated, throwing away quarters when she should have thought of a better lie when she had run into Michael in the hallway. This would have been the perfect time to have gotten into the lab. Still, since the mouse game was diverting, she went back to it. She was just choosing her cheese bonus when she was startled by an already familiar voice.

"What are you doing here?"

She looked up to see Jesse Crane, leaning casually against her machine. It made her uneasy to realize that his scent was provocative, and that he looked even better in his tailored shirt, khakis and sport jacket. When she glanced up, the bright green of his eyes against the bronze of his face was intense. She wouldn't want to face him at an inquiry, that was certain.

She wondered what it was about certain people that

made them instantly attractive. About certain *men,* she corrected herself, and the thought was even more disturbing. Michael Preston was definitely good-looking; Hugh was charming; Jack Pine exuded a quiet strength. But Jesse Crane... Just the sound of his voice seemed like a sexual stimulant. The least brush of his fingers spoke erotically to her innermost recesses. She was tempted to touch him, because just the feel of crisp fabric over muscled flesh would be arousing.

A blush was rising to her cheeks. She looked away from his eyes, but her gaze fell on his chest. And then below.

She closed her eyes.

"Hello?" he said softly.

What *was* she doing here? She forced herself to focus. To shake off the ridiculous sensation of instant seduction and sensuality.

Nothing, frankly, accomplishing nothing. "Um...gambling," she murmured.

She arched a brow, shrugging as she looked at him and hit the button on the machine again. "Losing money. What about you?"

He shrugged. "I live in the area."

"So do I, remember?"

"Who did you come with?"

"A group from Harry's."

"And who would that group be?"

"Michael, Jack and Hugh." She stared at the machine, trying not to let him see her mind working. "Are you out for a night on the town? Or just passing through?" Her machine did some binging and banging—three cheeses in a row. She had a return of ten dollars. Not bad.

"Why?" he asked.

"Just curious. Well, actually, if you're heading out…" She yawned, moving away from the machine. "I'm not much of a gambler. I was thinking of going back, but I came with the guys."

"I'll give you a ride," he told her. "Who should we tell you're leaving? Michael?"

"Um…any of them, I guess," she murmured. *Not Michael. He might get suspicious.* "Hugh is right there—we'll just tell him."

She slid off the stool, ready to head for Hugh's poker table.

"Aren't you forgetting something?" Jesse asked.

"What?"

"Your money."

"Oh. I didn't lose it all?"

"No. There's more than a hundred dollars there."

"Oh. Of course I want it," she said.

His eyes seemed to drill right through her. "Do you?" he inquired lightly. "I didn't think money means a thing to you."

She ignored him and gave her attention to the machine, hitting the "cash out" button.

"You have to wait for an attendant," he told her. "I'll let Hugh know you're leaving."

"Sure. Thanks."

The place was busy, the wait for an attendant long. She was ready to leave her winnings for some lucky stranger, she was so antsy, but she didn't know whether she was being watched. By the time they actually left, she fumed silently, the men might well be right behind them.

Finally, money stuffed into her bag, Lorena hurried past the slots and found Jesse waiting for her at the end of the row.

She quickly checked to make sure that the three men from the alligator farm were still at their tables.

They were.

"Sure you want to go?" Jesse inquired.

"Yes, thank you."

As they turned to leave, his set his palm against the small of her back, nothing more than a polite gesture. Even so, she felt that touch as if she had connected with a live electric current.

Outside, Jesse didn't speak as he politely seated her on the passenger side and slid behind the wheel.

She felt the silence.

"Thanks for taking me back," she said nervously.

"Not a problem."

Again there was silence. Uncomfortable silence. It should have been a casual drive. It wasn't. It felt as if the air between them was combustible.

"Is our casino a little too tame for you?" he asked at last.

"No. Honestly, I liked it a lot. All I ever play is slots, anyway. I don't understand craps, so it doesn't matter to me if there's a table or not. I guess I'm just not that much of a gambler."

"I'd say you were."

"Pardon?"

He glanced at her sharply. "Oh, you take chances. Racing out here like the wind. Working at Harry's. Going out with three men you've barely met. Especially when there have just been two truly gruesome murders in the area." His tone was amazingly matter-of-fact.

"I hardly think I'm in danger with my co-workers."

He didn't say any more until they had taken the turn into Harry's. She was digging in her purse for the pass that would open the door after hours when he startled her by leaning over and gripping her shoulder. The force was electric, and when she looked at him, she was certain she had guilt written all over her features.

"I really don't understand why you're lying to me. Or what makes you think I'm such a fool that I believe you. What are you doing here?" he demanded roughly.

"Working!"

"You know I'll have you checked out by morning," he said.

She prayed that he couldn't feel the trembling that was suddenly racing through her.

"Go right ahead. Check me out. I'm an R.N. You'll find that to be a fact." She reached for the door handle.

"You're playing with fire."

"I'm working. Earning a living."

"Two people, shot. I'd bet everything I have that the killer or killers didn't even know them. It was cold-blooded murder, as cold as it gets."

"Look, I know you're going to check me out. Believe me, you won't find a criminal record. I'm out here to work."

"Right." The green of his eyes was sharp, even in the dim light. "You've come down here to start over, start a new life, that's all."

"May I get out of the car now?"

He released her. The sudden loss of his touch created a chill.

Tell him the truth!

But she couldn't. She had nothing to go on. And he couldn't help, not if she couldn't offer him some kind of proof. And, anyway, could she be certain, absolutely certain, that he wasn't in any way involved?

Actually, yes. Somewhere deep inside, based on instinct, she simply knew the man was completely ethical.

But she didn't dare speak. He would send her packing.

"I'll tell you what you're not," he said softly.

"Oh?"

"A very good liar. So whatever you're up to, God help you."

She stared straight at him. "I am a registered nurse."

"And what else?"

"I dabbled in psychology, but a lot of those classes went toward the nursing degree."

"So you came down here to bandage knees and psychoanalyze the great American alligator?" he inquired dryly. "What else should I know about you?"

"There's this—I'm really tired," she told him.

"And stubborn as hell. You've barely arrived and everything has gone insane. So I'm going to hope that you're not dangerously stupid—or carelessly reckless."

She wondered how he could simply look at her and be able to read everything about her. Or was she that transparent to everyone?

It's just him, she thought with annoyance. Even when he wasn't touching her, it somehow felt as if he was. And even when he grilled her, she was tempted to lean closer to him, to do anything just to touch him, feel a sense of warmth. Even with so much at stake, no matter how she tried to control her mind, it kept running to thoughts of what it would be like just to lie beside him….

"May I get out of the car now?" She asked again, once more feeling drawn to tell him that she actually wanted to stay. Put her head on his shoulders. Tell him the whole truth. But she didn't dare.

"Well, I can't arrest you. At the moment." He turned away from her, shaking his dark head. "Good night, Ms. Fortier. And lock your door," he said.

"I intend to," she assured him, then exited the car as quickly as she could. Her fingers slipped on the little plastic ID entry card. She had to work it three times.

At last the door opened.

Jesse waited until she was inside, then drove away.

When he was gone, she didn't bother heading toward her own room. She walked straight to Michael Preston's lab. With no one around, she surprised herself with her ability to quickly pick the lock.

She knew it was dangerously stupid as she checked the big wall clock over the door, but she didn't stop. The hatchlings began to squeal the minute she entered the room.

Almost as if they sensed prey.

She ignored the sound and started with the desk drawers, then the computer. She knew that she would need a password to access his important files, but she hoped to study his general entries and discover whether he was involved or not.

The clock ticked as she worked. She read and read, keeping an eye on the clock.

Almost an hour since she had left the casino.

Regretfully, she turned off the computer and made a last survey to assure herself she'd left nothing out of order.

Then she left the room, quietly closing the door behind her. She listened for the lock to automatically slip into place.

Just in time. As she hurried down the hall, she heard voices. She quickly turned the corner, out of sight.

"If you're not bright enough to ask that woman out on a real date, I will."

Lorena recognized the voice. It was Hugh.

Michael answered, laughing dryly. "Yeah, well, I kind of thought that she was interested. But she lit out like a bat out of hell once Jesse arrived."

"She's not a poker player. One of us should have stayed with her."

"Is that it?" Michael said dryly. "Women *have* been known to find Jesse appealing."

"Yeah, and then they find out that they're lusting after the unobtainable."

"He won't be grieving forever," Michael said. "And either she went with him because she wanted to, or…"

"Or what?" Hugh demanded sharply.

"Or she wanted to get back here without the three of us."

She heard the rattle of the lab doorknob then. "Locked," he murmured.

"I'm asking her out," Hugh said. "For an airboat ride. That's innocent enough."

"Hey, every man for himself, huh?" Michael said.

Hugh laughed. "Yep, every man for himself."

She heard the lab door open and shut. Not knowing if Hugh had joined Michael or would be heading on down the hallway, Lorena fled.

As soon as she reached her own room, she thought of Jesse's warning and made sure her own door was locked.

Then she dragged a chair in front of it, wedging it tightly beneath the knob.

Still, it was a long time before she slept.

Jesse sat outside the alligator farm complex, watching. He'd left, parked on the embankment, and waited.

Once he'd seen Preston's car return, he'd counted the seconds carefully, then slipped his car back into gear to follow.

Just in the shadows, off the drive near the main entrance, he parked.

He spent the night in the car, his senses on alert.

The grunts of the gators, loud in the night, sounded now and then, sometimes just one or two, sometimes a cacophony.

Strange creatures. He'd been around them all his life. They were an amazing species, having survived longer than almost any other creature to have walked the earth.

Their calls and cries could be eerie, though.

He stayed until daybreak, waiting, though for what, he wasn't certain. Something. Some sign of danger.

Dawn broke. Light came softly, filling the horizon with pastels. There was a breeze. Birds cried and soared overhead.

He began to feel like a fool.

Then he heard the scream.

Chapter 6

Lorena bolted out of the bed, stunned and disoriented. The first sharp, staccato shriek that had awakened her had been followed by other screams and cries.

She threw on a robe and went flying out of her room, down the hall, and then burst out back to the ponds, the area from which the sounds of distress were still coming.

Then she heard the distant sound of sirens.

It was far too early for the gates to have opened to tourists, and she couldn't imagine what had happened. Her heart was thundering as she saw that most of the employees had gathered around the deep trench pond where Old Elijah was kept.

The biggest, meanest alligator in the place.

At first she stood on the periphery of the crowd, trying to ascertain what had happened, listening to the shouts that rose around her.

"How in hell did *he* fall in?" one of the waitresses asked, incredulous.

"Roger has been a guard here from the beginning…what would make him lean far enough over to fall in?" asked one of the ticket-takers.

"Jesse's in there now. He'll get him out," a feminine voice said.

Lorena swung around to see that Sally Dickerson was there, threading her fingers through her long red hair. She turned to stare at Lorena. Where everyone else seemed to have eyes filled with concern, Sally's had a gleam. She was enjoying the excitement.

"What?" Lorena said.

"Jesse's gone in. He'll get Roger out."

Lorena wasn't sure who she pushed out of the way then, but she rushed to the concrete rim of the great dipped pond and natural habitat that held Old Elijah.

There was a man on the ground, next to the concrete wall. Jack Pine and Hugh Humphrey were there at the side of the wall, maneuvering some kind of rope-rigged gurney down to the fallen guard, who was apparently unconscious.

There was Jesse.

And there was Old Elijah.

The way the habitat was set up, there was the concrete wall and rim, a pond area, and then a re-creation of a wet-land hummock.

The great alligator had so far remained on the other side of the water. He watched with ancient black eyes as Jesse Crane moved with care to manipulate the body of the fallen guard with the greatest care possible onto the gurney.

Jesse was no fool. He kept his eye on the alligator the whole time.

"Where the hell is Harry with that tranq gun?" Jack demanded hoarsely.

"Got him!" Jesse shouted. "Haul him up, haul him up!"

Tense, giving directions to one another as they brought up the gurney, the men were careful to raise it without unbalancing the unconscious figure held in place by buckled straps. Jesse helped guide the gurney until it was over his head.

And all the time, Old Elijah watched.

Motionless, still as death, only the eyes alive.

Others jumped in to help as the gurney rose. Jesse reached for the rope ladder that he'd come down and started up.

And then Old Elijah moved.

He was like a bullet, a streak of lightning. Someone screamed.

The massive jaws opened.

They snapped shut.

They caught the tail end of the rope ladder, and the great head of the beast began to thrash back and forth.

Jesse, nearing the top, teetered dangerously. A collective cry rose; then he caught the rim of the concrete barrier and hauled himself over.

At the same time, they heard the whistle of a shot.

Harry had arrived, holding a huge tranquilizer gun on his shoulder.

The dart struck Old Elijah on the shoulder.

At first, it was as if a fly had landed on his back, nothing more.

The gator backed away, drawing the remnants of the rope ladder with him. Then, as if he were some type of blow-up toy with the air seeping from him, Old Elijah fell. The eyes that had blazed with such an ancient predatory fervor went blank.

The crowd was cheering Jesse; med techs were racing up, and more officers had arrived to control the space and let the emergency techs work.

Jack slammed a hand on Jesse's shoulder. Hugh shook his head and fell back against the barrier, relieved.

Jesse looked down into the enclosure, shaking his head as he stared at Old Elijah. Then his gaze rose, almost instinctively, and met Lorena's.

She stared back, oddly frightened to see the way his eyes narrowed as he regarded her, filled with suspicion. His mouth was hard. She flushed; he didn't look away.

Someone caught his attention, and he turned.

"Damn, Harry, it took you long enough to get that gun," Jack called, shaking his head.

"Jack Pine, you're the damned handler, so get a handle on what happened here," Harry shouted back.

"Calm down. We're going to have an inquiry," Jesse said.

"Inquiry?" Harry snorted. "Roger was out here by himself. What the fool was doing leaning over the concrete, I don't know. We'll just have to wait until he's regained consciousness to find out."

"Yeah, *if* he regains consciousness," Jack snorted. He was tense, and his features were hard as he stared at Harry.

"Hell of a thing—" Harry began, and then realized that he had an audience, more than a dozen employees hanging around. He stopped speaking and shook his head again. "This show's over, folks. Back to work, everybody back to work." Then he turned to Jesse. "Hell, Jesse, what kind of questions could anybody have?"

"That will come later. I'm getting in the ambulance copter with Roger," Jesse said, brushing past Harry.

He stared at Lorena again then. His features remained taut and grim, and his eyes now held...

A warning?

He hesitated, speaking to a couple of officers who had arrived along with the med techs, then hurried after the stretcher.

A man in one of the Miccosukee force uniforms spoke up, his voice calm and reassuring, yet filled with authority. "Go ahead, folks, get going. We'll be speaking with you all one by one."

The crowd slowly began to disperse. Harry was complaining to the officer. "I don't get it. What could your questions be? For some fool reason, Roger got stupid and leaned too far over the barrier. No one else was out here. Security was his job."

"Harry, we have to ask questions," the officer said. "Hey, if there were an outsider in here, giving Roger or anyone a problem, you'd want to know, right?"

"Well, yeah," Harry said, as if the idea had just occurred to him. "You boys go right ahead. Question everyone. Damned right, I'd want to know."

He turned to walk away, then saw that several of his employees hadn't left.

"Get going, folks. It's a workday, and this isn't a charity. So get to work. And everyone, give these officers your fullest cooperation." Then he walked away himself, followed by one of the officers.

Lorena nearly jumped a mile when she felt a hand on her shoulder. She swung around. Michael was there, looking sleepy, concerned but foggy, also clad in a robe.

"What the hell happened?"

She explained.

He shook his head. "Well, that's about as weird as it gets. Roger has been here forever. He should have known better."

"Would that alligator…Old Elijah…would he have eaten the man, do you think?" Lorena queried softly.

"He's really well fed, so…who knows," Michael said. "Eaten him? Maybe. More likely he just would have gotten angry, taken a bite, tossed him around, drowned him. Who knows. I don't question Old Elijah. There's only one thing I can say with certainty about alligators."

"And that is?"

Michael's eyes met hers directly. "That you'll never really know anything about them," he said flatly. "You'll never know what goes on behind the evil in those eyes."

Jesse sat in the back of the emergency helicopter, doing his best to keep out of the way of the men desperately working to save Roger's life. He didn't need to ask questions, not that they would be heard above the roar of the blades, not from where he sat. A glance at the med tech who had taken the man's vitals and affixed his IV line told him that Roger had not regained consciousness.

As soon as they reached the hospital, Jesse paced the emergency room waiting lounge. Hell of a place. He knew the hospital was good; one of the best in the nation for trauma. But it was also the place where those without insurance came for help, and the place was thick with the ill, the injured and those who had brought them.

He wasn't the only law enforcement officer there. As he waited, two drug overdoses and a man with a knife in his back were rushed in, escorted by cops. Strange place, he thought. Stranger here, in the heart of the city, than out in the Glades. The wealth to be found in the area was astounding; movie stars, rock stars and celebrities of all kinds had multimillion dollar mansions out on the islands, in the Gables and scattered throughout the county. At the same time, refugees from Central and South America abounded, many who slept under bridges, or lived in the crack houses that could be found not so far from the million-dollar mansions.

At length, one of the doctors came out. "Well, we've got him stabilized. But he's in a coma. He's not going to be talking."

"Will he come out of it?" Jesse asked.

"I don't know," the doctor told him honestly.

Jesse nodded, and handed the doctor his business card.

"I'll call you first thing, and I mean first thing, if there's any change at all," the doctor promised.

Jesse thanked him. There was a Florida Highway Patrol officer in the waiting room who had just finished with an accident victim. He offered to drive Jesse back. It was a long way, and Jesse thanked him for the offer.

"Heard you've been having some bad business around here," the officer, Tom Hennesy, said as they drove. "Anything new on those shootings?"

"No. Metro-Dade Homicide is handling that case, though."

Hennesy nodded. "You had a fatal gator attack, too."

Jesse nodded.

"Strange, huh?" Hennesy said. "Usually that kind of thing only happens when someone wanders into the wrong place." He shrugged. "Of course, the 'wrong' place is getting harder to avoid these days, what with developers eating up the Everglades. Still, it's usually only the big gators that will attack an adult. It's usually toddlers. Or pets." He cast a sideways glance at Jesse and flushed slightly. "I was reading up after the attack the other day. Since 1948, there have been fewer than 350 attacks on humans in this state, and the number of fatal attacks is only in the teens." He laughed. "I remember when the creatures were endangered, and when the first alligator farm opened in 1985. My uncle used to come out to the Glades, sit in a cabin and drink beer, and go out and hunt gators—till they made the endangered list. And now… My wife wanted to move close to the water. Now, after the latest incident, she wants to move out of state and up into the mountains somewhere."

Jesse smiled at the man, offering what he hoped was polite empathy.

"Hell, you're down here all the time," Hennesy said. "Think about it. How many attacks have you seen?"

Jesse looked at him. "Well, my uncle Pete lost a thumb, but he was one of the best wrestlers the village down there ever had. He was proud of it, actually. I don't think you can call that an attack, though."

When they at last reached the alligator farm, Jesse was disturbed to realize that more than half the day was gone.

The place was full of tourists, as if nothing had happened. A discreet inquiry assured him that Lorena was busy, helping out with Michael Preston's hatchling speeches.

He took a glance into the lab and saw that there were at least twenty people on the current tour. Lorena didn't see him. He watched her, watched the way she smiled, seemingly at ease. But in reality she was moving around the lab looking for something, he realized. She was subtle, leaning against a cabinet, a desk, casually assessing the contents, but she was definitely searching for something.

He was tempted to shout at her. *Stupid!*

Was she stupid, or dangerously reckless? Why? What was driving her?

A little while later, when he drove away from the farm, he realized that he'd been afraid to leave, afraid to head home for a shower. He was tired as hell, but the shower was necessary. Sleep would have to wait.

Lorena heard that Jesse had returned to Harry's. That he had spoken with a number of people.

Just not her.

The next morning she met Thorne Thiessen, the veterinarian. He had come to take a look at Old Elijah.

He was a distinguished-looking man, weather-worn, with a pleasant disposition, very tall, very fit. He had his assistant with him, a huge guy named John Smith. They both looked like extremely powerful men, in exceptional shape.

Maybe that was a requirement for survival in the swamp. Or else something in the genetics of the men in the area.

Watching Thiessen examine Old Elijah had been a real education. They had pulled out a lot of equipment—Elijah was one big beast—and they had snared him, something that had taken Jack Pine, Hugh, John Smith and two part-time wranglers to manage. The gator had thrashed, even when caught, and sent several of the handlers flying. Between them, however, they got the creature still, with Jack making the leap to the animal's back, shutting the great jaw and taping it closed.

Only then did Thiessen go into the pit. He took blood samples, checked the crocodilian's eyes, did some kind of a temperature reading and checked out his hide.

Despite the time she'd spent in school, Lorena really didn't know how the vet was determining if the ancient creature was in good health or not. Personally, she thought that the way he had been able to toss grown men around as if they were weightless seemed to prove that he was doing okay.

Jesse showed up right when Thiessen was leaving. Lorena, who had been watching from the pit area, did her best to eavesdrop. The men greeted each other cordially enough, but then Jesse pressed the vet, who in turn became defensive.

"I'm working on it, Jesse. But come on, Homicide doesn't see any connection between the alligator limb and the murders. Something ate the rest of the thing, that's all. Poachers don't kill people with high-powered rifles."

Jesse shrugged. "I can see where this may not be at the top of your priority list, but it *is* high on mine. If you don't want to deal with the responsibility, I can just take it to the FBI lab."

Thorne frowned, even more indignant. "No one knows reptiles the way that I do!"

"That's why I brought the specimen to you. Another day or so, Thorne, then I'm going to have to go for second best."

As he finished speaking, Lorena realized that he'd noticed she was there. She had forgotten to eavesdrop discreetly.

But there were others around, too. Jack and Hugh were speaking together, just a few feet away. Sally was standing politely to the rear, obviously waiting for a chance to have a word with Jesse.

Even Harry was still by the pit, calling out orders to the two wary part-time handlers, who had been left to free Old Elijah from the tape on his snout.

Michael Preston was there, too, sipping coffee with a thoughtful frown as he watched all the activity.

Jesse, however, was gazing thoughtfully at *her.*

"Ms. Fortier," he murmured. "I need to see you later," he said.

He turned to leave. Sally tapped him on the arm, asking a question that Lorena couldn't hear. As Jesse walked away, Sally was still at his side.

"Hey!" Harry called. "Doors are opening."

Lorena realized that although she was always distracted when she brought visitors through Michael's lab, she actually enjoyed his talks. He had a nice flair for the dramatic. That morning, though, she felt the frustration of not being able to find anything out of the ordinary. Except for the eggs with the cracked shells. That was where changes—or *enhancements*—might take place. But they were out in the open. Part of the show.

In the afternoon, she watched as Jack and Hugh both put on their own demonstrations. Jack wrestled a six foot gator to the amusement of the crowd. Hugh brought out gators in various stages of growth, thrilling the children, who were allowed to touch the animals. After the last show, Hugh approached her.

"How about an airboat ride? See some of the scenery up close and personal?" he suggested, his grin charming and hopeful.

She agreed, and soon, they were out in the Glades. She had been afraid, at first, when it had looked as if they were trying to take off over solid ground. But it wasn't ground at all.

The river of grass. That was what it was and exactly the

way it looked. As they traveled, Hugh educated her about their environs, shouting to be heard over the motor. The Everglades really wasn't a swamp but a constantly moving river; it was simply that the rate at which the water moved was so slow that it wasn't discernible to the naked eye.

Hugh obviously loved the area. Before they started out, he had explained that he was an Aussie; would always be an Aussie at heart, but that he had come to love this place as home.

Trees on hummocks seemed to rush by with tremendous speed. Ahead of them, brilliantly colored birds, large and small, burst out of the water and into the sky. At last Hugh cut the motor, and the airboat came to rest in the middle of what seemed like a strange and forgotten expanse of endless water, space and humid heat.

"So how do you like the airboat?" Hugh asked. He had a cooler in the rear of the boat and edged around carefully to open it. He produced two bottles of beer.

She accepted one.

"The feel of the wind is great," she told him.

He took a seat again, grinning as he looked at her. "You like it out here?"

"It's strange. A bit to get used to. But yes. I don't think I've ever seen more magnificent birds. Not even in a zoo."

"Around the early 1900s, some of them were hunted into extinction. Their feathers were needed for every stylish hat," Hugh said, leaning back. "But they *are* fabulous, aren't they?"

She nodded. "So, Hugh, were you a croc hunter back home in the Outback?"

He laughed. "Actually, I was born and raised in Sydney, but I always wanted to find out about the wilds. We've got some beautiful country at home, but there's just something here…the loneliness, the trees, the birds, the…I don't know. Some people simply fall in love with the land. Despite the SST-size mosquitoes, the venomous snakes and the alligators."

"Have you been a handler ever since you got here?" she asked. "I mean, did you ever help with the research side of things?"

He laughed. "Research?" He shook his head. "I know enough about gators without that. I know when they mate, know that a mother gator is one of the fiercest creatures known to man. And I know about the jaws, and that's what counts."

He sat back easily, adjusting his hat. He was attentive and clearly glad to be with her. In fact, he really seemed like a nice guy.

And he knew nothing about research.

Or so he claimed.

But here they were, in the middle of nowhere, and if he had wanted to cause her any harm…

"Damn!" he said suddenly.

"What?" she asked.

He lifted his beer, indicating something west of them. She peered in that direction, squinting, trying to see what he was seeing.

She realized that there was an embankment, and that they were in a canal. Trees grew at the water's edge, and it seemed that there was a small hummock in the direction he was pointing.

Limbs were down here and there, no doubt a result of the early summer rainstorms she had heard came frequently here.

"There… They really are amazing creatures. They blend

perfectly with their environment," Hugh said, his voice a whisper touched with awe. "See him?"

Suddenly she did. Just the eyes and a hint of the nose were visible above the water. And then, way behind the head, she could see the slight rise of the back.

"He's huge!" Hugh continued softly. "I've never seen one that big. I've never even seen a croc that big."

"How can you tell his size?" she asked, whispering, too, though she didn't know why. Actually, she did, she realized. She didn't want to attract the creature's attention.

"Well," Hugh said, if you look at the water—"

"The water looks black," she protested.

He laughed softly. "It's not the water, it's the vegetation. But look closely. You can see the length of the body. We're talking huge. Maybe twenty-something feet."

"They don't get that big here!" she heard herself protest.

As they watched, the alligator suddenly submerged. Lorena felt a sharp stab of fear, sudden and primitive. She was certain that the creature was coming for them.

The airboat was small and built for two, with both seats at the rear. The nose of the vehicle offered only a small bit of space for supplies. The boat was fairly flat-bottomed, and it would be hard to knock over, but...

How much could a creature like that weigh?

"Man, I would have liked to see him up close," Hugh marveled.

Lorena couldn't speak. She was certain that Hugh was going to get his wish, that the gator would be there, beneath them, in a matter of seconds.

Frowning, Hugh rose. Despite the rocking of the airboat, he moved easily and confidently. She was about to scream to him to sit down, that he needed his gun, that...

She heard it then. The motor of another airboat.

Just then something brushed by their boat. Just touching it. Nosing it.

Testing it?

Then the other airboat came into the picture, whipping over the water. It was a much larger vehicle, with the motor and giant fan far in the rear, and with more storage space and six seats in front of the helm. She noticed that it bore a tribal insignia.

Then she saw Jesse.

She released a long breath, aware that she wasn't afraid anymore, that even his airboat seemed to shout of authority.

The creature had disappeared; it was no longer touching their airboat.

"Hey!" Jesse shouted, cutting his motor as his vehicle drew next to theirs.

"Hey, Jesse," Hugh said dryly. It was apparent that his romantic plans had just been shattered.

"What are you two doing out here?" Jesse asked with a frown.

Hugh cocked his head, his hands on his hips. "I asked the lady out, and she agreed."

Jesse looked impatient. "Hugh, I don't know how you missed my notice. We've got a man-eater out here. We're going to get a group of hunting guides out here and go after it. The medical examiner says that Billy Ray was bushwhacked by one big son of a bitch. We're going after it. It's not safe out here right now."

Hugh snorted. "Jesse, I've been dealing with gators for half my life. I'm armed, and I can take care of Lorena. I carry more than one big gun."

Jesse shook his head. "Hugh, you're one of the best. But

Billy Ray knew alligators, too. Take your airboat on back. Lorena, step over here."

"Now, wait a minute!" Hugh protested. "Lorena is with me."

"She's coming in for questioning," Jesse said.

"What?" she and Hugh asked simultaneously.

Those startling green eyes leveled upon her hard. "Lorena needs to answer some questions about an incident at the alligator farm the other day."

"Jesse, you are crazy—" Lorena began.

"I can put the cuffs on you," he assured her.

"What the hell are you talking about?" Hugh demanded.

Jesse leveled his eyes on Lorena as he answered Hugh's question. "Something to do with a little kid getting a bite. I'm sure Harry wants it kept quiet. Therefore, I need a few answers."

Hugh frowned, staring at Lorena. "You don't have to go with him. What are you trying to pull here, Jesse Crane?" Hugh demanded.

"I think that Lorena wants to come with me," Jesse said, staring at her meaningfully.

Her skin prickled. It wasn't with the kind of panic she had felt when she believed that a monster gator was stalking her, but with an overwhelming sense of unease. *He knew.*

And maybe he was giving her a chance to talk to him before he blew the whistle on her.

She sighed, rising. The boat rocked.

"There was a bit of a problem with one of the children the other morning, Hugh. Easily taken care of. I'll just go with Jesse now," she said smoothly.

Panic seized her once again when she was ready to step from boat to boat. Where had the gator gone?"

Whatever ruffled male feathers had begun to fly, the situation was suddenly eased as Hugh, holding her arm as she moved to join Jesse, said, "I think we just saw your alligator."

"Here?" Jesse asked.

There was about a foot and a half of empty space between the boats as they rocked gently in the water. Lorena looked down.

Her heart slammed into her throat.

There it was. Submerged, and moving in fluid silence, just beneath the surface.

She nearly threw herself into Jesse's arms.

"There!" she said. "Underneath us."

He frowned at her, dark brows drawn, eyes narrowed. He forced her into a seat and strode back to the edge of the airboat. "Where? Hugh, you see it?"

Hugh was also searching the water. He had a shotgun in the back of the airboat. He reached for it and stood still, watching.

Time passed.

It felt like an eternity to Lorena, who heard the drone of a mosquito but was afraid to move, too frozen even to swat at the creature.

At last Jesse sighed.

"It might have been here, but I don't see it now," he said. "But this might well be its territory, so we'll start here tomorrow."

"Sunset?" Hugh asked.

"Right before. You gonna join us?"

"Yeah," Hugh said. "I travel around here all the time, though. I haven't seen that gator before."

"What was left of Billy Ray's body was tangled in the

trees not too far from here. You know, right around the bend, where he had his favorite fishing spot. Yes, this is its territory. I'll pick you up at Harry's, six o'clock sharp tomorrow evening."

Jesse started up his motor.

The sound was like the sudden whirr of a thousand birds, rising from the swamp.

She gripped her chair, still feeling cold. Hugh waved.

She couldn't wave back.

The wind lashed around her, whipping her hair around her face. She closed her eyes.

She was startled when the motor died, along with the forward motion of the boat.

She opened her eyes. They still seemed to be in the middle of nowhere.

There was a hummock where they had come to rest, land that wasn't covered in the deceptive saw grass that grew where the water ran, making a person believe that there was terra firma beneath.

And yet in all directions, she still saw only wilderness.

There was no sound, except for the cries of birds, the rustle of foliage.

She swallowed, frowned, and stared at Jesse uneasily.

"Where are we?"

"My place," he said. "And you can talk to me here, tell me the truth, or we'll just head downtown, to the FBI office. Here's your chance, Lorena. Truth or dare. What do you know, and what the hell are you really doing here?"

Chapter 7

Despite the fact that there was a well-maintained dock, Jesse could see that Lorena was more than a bit concerned about where they were going when he helped her out of the airboat.

His house had been built on a hummock and, he thought, combined the best of tradition and the modern world. There were still members of his tribe who made their homes in chickees, but for the most part, beyond the village and the other tourist stops, tribal members lived in normal houses, concrete block and stucco, sturdy structures that offered the same comforts as those enjoyed by everyone else.

He was lucky to own the land, which had been his father's. And it was a good stretch of hummock, rich with trees and foliage, and high enough to keep it from flooding during hurricanes or the rainy season. As they came in from the rear, winding along the path from the canal, the

first sight was a chickee. Chickees had first come into
being when various tribes—once grouped together under
the term "Seminoles"—had moved deep into the Everglades to escape persecution and the white determination
to export every last Native American to the western reser-
vations. High above the ground, the chickee offered pro-
tection from snakes and gators. The open sides allowed the
breezes to pass through continually, keeping the inhabitants
cool year round.

Lorena gave the chickee a nervous glance, and he saw
the relief on her face when they rounded a bend and she
saw the house.

There was a screened-in patio with a pool, and sliding
glass doors that led from it into the house. He owned a fairly
typical ranch-style dwelling, with the large rear, "Florida
room" extending the width of the back. He had a good en-
tertainment center and comfortable sofas and chairs, which
often led to him being the one to host Sunday football get-
togethers. His home probably differed from some in that it
was filled with Indian artifacts: Miccosukee, Seminole and
others, including South American and Inuit. He had totem
poles, lances, spears, shields and buffalo skulls, all artisti-
cally—at least in his mind—arranged, and he had come to
love the feeling that he was surrounded by both past and
present, tradition and the need for all Americans to be aware
of the modern world. He considered education the most
necessary tool for any Native American, and finding the path
between prosperity and ethnicity was not an easy one.

"Thank God for bingo," he murmured aloud.

"What?"

Her eyes were wide; he could tell that she was decidedly
uncomfortable, yet apparently relieved at the same time.

"Coffee? Tea? Soda? Beer or wine?" he asked. "Sorry, that's all I keep around." He left her standing in the Florida room and walked through the hall, hanging a quick left into the kitchen, where a bypass over the counter opened to allow him to keep an eye on her.

She shook her head uneasily. "I'm fine."

"Then I'll have coffee."

He reached into the cupboards for the paraphernalia he needed, watching her as he did so.

Some of the trepidation in her face had eased. She was walking around, studying the various pieces on the walls. She turned suddenly, as if feeling him watching her.

"Have you always lived here?" she asked, trying to sound casual.

"In the general area, yes. This house is new, though."

"Ah."

"And, let's see…you were raised in Jacksonville. Attended the University of Florida. Where you did indeed earn a nursing degree."

"Yes," she murmured, looking away.

"And a law degree."

Her eyes flew to his again. Belligerent, defensive.

"All right, so I've spent the last few years with a law firm. My nursing credentials are still good. You seem to know everything, so you must know that, too."

"I do," he assured her grimly. "Sure you don't want a cup of coffee?"

"All right," she murmured.

She walked around to join him in the kitchen. He wondered how she could have spent the late afternoon in an airboat in the swamp and still manage to retain such an alluring scent.

"Sugar...cream," he said, indicating the containers.

She added a touch of cream to her cup, not looking at him. Her fingers were shaking as she stirred, but she quickly returned to the Florida room, taking a seat on one of the sofas that looked out over the pool.

"All right," he said, taking a seat next to her. "We need to start communicating here. This is serious. Shall I continue, or do you just want to talk to me?"

"You're going to try to get me out of here," she said, not looking at him. Then her eyes shot to his. "And I'm not inept. Actually, I'm a crack shot."

"Your life seems filled with accomplishments," he said with obvious irony.

She blushed, looking away. "I thought I wanted to go into nursing...but then I wound up taking some legal courses related to medical ethics and I found out that I liked the law. I was able to work part-time in a hospital while I went back to college. I was lucky. My dad was associated with a firm that was known for going to bat for the underdog. They hired me right out of law school."

"Which has nothing to do with why you're here," he said softly.

"Actually, in a way it does," she murmured, staring down again. Then she looked up at him. "One thing about studying the law is that you learn you need proof to go to court."

He shook his head, looking at her, then taking the cup from her and setting it on the coffee table. He took both her hands. "All right, here's the rest of what I know. You're going under the name Fortier because that was your mother's maiden name. Your father was Dr. Eugene Duval, working for Eco-smart, a company that, among other facilities, ran an alligator farm. He died last year after a fall down a stairway. So why does that bring you here?"

She shook her head. "He didn't fall."

"Lorena, I've read the police reports. He was alone in the building at the time."

"No. He did *not* just fall."

Jesse sighed, squeezing her hands. "Lorena, I know what it's like to desperately seek something behind the obvious. Your father fell down a stairway. He broke his neck."

"No," she said stubbornly.

"Why are you so convinced it wasn't an accident?"

"Because he had something. Something that his killer wanted."

"And that was?" Jesse persisted.

She hesitated, realizing that he didn't know everything.

He squeezed her hands more tightly. The lingering scent of her cologne wafted around him, seemed to permeate his system. He realized that his own heart was pounding, that the blood was rushing in a hot wave through his system. He was torn between the desire to gently touch her face and the equally strong desire to draw her into his arms, shake her, tell her none of this was worth her life.

He desperately wanted to hold her. And more. The texture of her skin was suddenly so fascinating that he longed to explore it with the tips of his fingers. Her features were so delicate, elegant and determined that he was tempted to test them with the palm of his hand.

He fought the desire that had begun to build in his system the first time he had seen her. She was angry, lost, determined…and trusting. He knew he should pull his hands away. He didn't. He couldn't. He had to get answers from her—now.

"Lorena, what did your father have?" he demanded.

She stared back at him, clenching her teeth; then she shook her head. "You mean you don't know? It's obvious. He had a formula."

"A formula for what?"

"Well, basically, steroids," she said flatly. "There were other ingredients, but the formula was based on steroids." She inhaled, exhaled, looking away but not drawing away. "My father was a great man. He wanted to feed the world. He worked with all kinds of animals, trying to find a way to improve the amount and quality of their meat without creating the chemical dangers you so often find in farmed meats. He saw alligators as the wave of the future. A creature that had been endangered—nearly wiped off the face of the earth—then raised in captivity to return with a vengeance. In his mind, we were going to be looking to a number of basically new food sources, new to the American public, at least. Emu. Beefalo. Different fish. Eels. And alligators. He thought they were magnificent creatures, with hides that could be used for all kinds of things and meat that could be improved in taste, quality and quantity. So he began working on a formula. Now he's dead and someone else has it—and I think Harry's place may be involved."

Jesse stared at her blankly, wondering why something like this hadn't occurred to him. *Because it was right out of a science fiction novel, that was why.*

"Lots of people work with alligators," he said, his tone sharper than he had intended. "Lots of scientists work with formulas to improve breeding and supply."

"Maybe, but my father had found one that improved the creatures' size to such an extent that…that he destroyed his own specimens."

Jesse felt frozen for a moment. It was all beginning to make sense. Too much sense. He was accustomed to drug-related crimes in the Everglades, or illegal immigrants, and the big money and guns that came with both. He knew the tragedy of greed, gangs, and the jealousy and fury behind domestic violence, and the tribulations brought on by the abuse of alcohol. And now industrial espionage might well be exactly what they were looking for. *A formula that was dangerous, but that could take a business to the top of the heap?* It made way too much sense. A couple killed for what appeared to be nothing had probably seen something they shouldn't see. A man who knew the Glades like the back of his hand, dead, killed by an alligator. But what kind of an alligator? Perhaps one scientifically induced to grow bigger—and more dangerous?

"All right, your father was working on a formula, but he's been dead for more than a year. There are all kinds of establishments working with alligators, all through Florida, Georgia, Texas and more. What brought you here?" he asked.

She hesitated. "I finally cleaned out all my dad's business communications. An old e-mail I found from Harry's Alligator Farm and Museum seemed to point in this direction."

"Was Harry Rogers ever in Jacksonville? Did he know your father?"

She shook her head. "Not that I know of."

"I assume your father communicated with a lot of other institutions."

"Yes, but…none of the others were…well, located in such a wilderness. A place where it's possible to hide so much."

"Exactly what did the e-mail say, and who was it from?"

"I don't know. It wasn't signed. It was just a query, but

there was something off about it. Something greedy. My father wrote back that he couldn't help."

"Then…?"

"It came right after there had been an article about my dad that mentioned the kind of research he was doing. So I came here, and…that couple got killed, and you found a piece of an alligator there, and then that poor man was… eaten."

"Still…"

"Jesse, I'm telling you, there was nothing else to go on, nothing."

"What about the other employees where your dad worked? What did they say?"

She shook her head in disgust. "According to everyone, my father had destroyed his research, the formula and his specimens. He worked for a very aboveboard corporation. When he said his research had taken a dangerous turn, they gave him the freedom to start over. So now they're all sorry, and they all understand that I'm upset. But as far as they're concerned, it was an accident."

She stared at him, then grasped his hands. "But it *wasn't* an accident. I know it. Harry—or someone here—got my father's formula, and they killed him to do it. You have to believe me! And now they've lost a few of their specimens, and those gators are running around the Glades killing people. They're trying to track them down, but they don't want to get caught, and I think that's why your friends were killed. Whoever was out there picking up the specimen decided that Hector and Maria had seen too much. But what really scares me is that I think they're still trying to use the formula. Jesse, please, think about it. You said that Hector and Maria were wonderful people, that they couldn't have been drug-running. So you have to go to the next conclusion—that they were killed for something they saw, for what they might know. Come on! Why else would anyone kill your friends? They were shot because they saw the alligator. And the killers dared to murder them because they knew everyone would just assume it had something to do with drugs. Jesse, I'm right, and you know it."

He drew away from her at last, then stood and walked to the glass doors, looking out at the pool and the deep, rich green of the hummock beyond, not seeing. "Lorena, your dad has been dead more than a year, right?" he said softly.

"Right."

"And his research went back several years. But alligators, even pampered hatchlings, only grow about a foot a year. To get a creature big enough to kill a man would take well over a decade."

"Jesse, you don't understand just what can be done once man starts messing with nature. My father began his studies about five years ago, and with the alterations he could create, a gator could grow as much as four feet in a year. You figure it out. Do the math. See where we'd be right now," she said softly.

"I don't believe it," he said, but he wondered, *Was it possible?*

"You've got to get out of here," he said flatly. "This is about the wildest theory I've heard in my entire life, but if there's any truth in it whatsoever, someone is going to find out who you are. You've got to get away." He spun on her. "And another thing. Why the hell didn't you tell me about this when you arrived down here?"

"Hey! The second time I ever saw you, you were *at*

Harry's. Sally told me you come there all the time. How could I know for certain that you weren't involved somehow?"

He sighed, looking down. "I'm a cop, Lorena. And just like I said at the beginning—a real one."

She rose, staring back at him. "And you're going to tell me that there haven't been dirty cops?"

He lifted his hands; then his eyes narrowed, and he strode over to her, taking her by the shoulders, ready to shake her for real. His fingers tensed where he held her, his teeth locked. He fought both his temper and his fears for her. At last he said, "You couldn't tell? You couldn't tell by *getting to know me* that I wasn't crooked?"

She inhaled, staring at him, eyes wide. She parted her lips, ready to speak, but words didn't come. She moistened her lips, ready to speak again, then just shook her head and, to his surprise, leaned it against him.

He wrapped his arms around her. Time ticked away as they stood there and he felt the soft force of her body against his, his own emotions washing through him with the force of a tidal wave. Heat began to fill him. He was torn, ready to rush out and pound his fist into anyone who would so coldly kill and let loose such a danger. But he was a police officer, sworn to uphold the law. He'd been a detective, trained to find out the truth before ripping into something like a maniac.

But he was also simply a man.

And here *she* was, in his arms. She had elicited emotion and longing in him from the first time he had seen the green-and-gold magic in her eyes, heard the tone of her voice. He'd been irritated, angered, enchanted. He'd seen the empathy in her eyes for others, the spark of fire when she was angry.

This wasn't the time.

He had taken her away from Hugh, and Hugh would be angry now, telling the tale to everyone.

And at Harry's, they might be suspicious....

"You can't go back there," he said, and he lifted her chin, his thumb playing over the flesh of her cheek.

Her eyes met his. Her fingers moved down his back, dancing lightly along the length of his spine. "I *have* to go back," she whispered.

"No," he said. And he brought his lips to hers. She didn't protest or hesitate for a second. It was as if they had both been simmering, awaiting the boiling point, and when they touched at last…

She melted into his arms, breasts and hips fitting neatly into his form. Her fingers threaded into his hair; her mouth tasted of mint and fire.

They broke apart. "I have to…" she said, and her meaning was unclear, because they fused together again, and her hands worked down to his hips, then below, cupping his buttocks, drawing him closer.

At last he caressed her face as he had longed to, exploring texture and shape. Then his fingers fell to the buttons of her shirt, and the fabric obediently parted. His fingers slid along the flesh of her throat, stroked, then careered down the length of her neck. Beneath the cotton of her shirt, he found her bra strap, slipped it away, and his lips dropped to her shoulder, while his fingers continued to disrobe her, baring more flesh for the eager whisper of his tongue. He felt her hands at his belt, then realized his gun was there. He released her long enough to discard his gun belt, then drew her back quickly, fevered, heedless of anything then but the wanting and the heady knowledge that she was just as hungry as he was.

Her skirt and delicate lace bra fell to the floor, and the sleek length of her back was available to be savored by the touch of his fingers, while his lips found the hollows at her collarbone, then moved steadily down, finding her breasts. He felt the quickening of her breath, and that, too, was an aphrodisiac. She was smooth and soft, erotic, hot, vibrant. Her lips and teeth on his shoulders, bathing, biting, aroused him. Her hands, deft and seductive, were at the waistband of his trousers. It was then he realized that, remote as his house might be, the glass panes opened to the glory of the Everglades—and the eyes of anyone who might wander by. He caught her up into his arms, heedless of the clothing they left scattered behind, and strode down the hallway to his bedroom. As he did so, her eyes met his, dazed and mercurial, fascinating, poignant pools. And then her fingers swept back a dark lock of his hair, touching his face as he had so tenderly touched hers.

Night was coming to the Everglades. Coming in hues of crimson and purple, red and gold. The light shone dimly into the room, illuminating them as they fell onto the bed and came together again in a fury of naked flesh. Every little nuance of her seemed to touch and awaken and arouse him. Whispers and soft moans escaped her lips, a siren's song, as he reveled in the discovery of her, the tautness of her abdomen, the length of her legs, the firm fullness of her breasts. And in return…her hands were on him, touching without restraint, fingers no more than a whisper, and then a tease that brought the blood thundering through his veins again, his own breath a drumbeat, the tension in him unbearable.

And yet the anguish was sweet. As if the moment would not come again and had to be cherished, savored. He felt he died a thousand little deaths, not willing to allow it to end, hands upon her everywhere, lips tasting, teasing, giving homage, demanding response. He held himself above her, found her mouth, his tongue thrusting within, gentle at first, then almost angry. Finally he allowed his body to slide slowly against hers as he eased himself lower, again finding the fullness of her breasts, the rose-tipped peaks of her nipples, and below, his tongue stroking a rib, delving into her naval, the lean, low skin of her midriff, then…a kneecap, outer thigh, inner thigh, and the crux of her sex.

He heard the anxious, heady sound of her whispers and moans, protest, encouragement. She writhed against him and into him, and he felt the pulse of her body, until at last he rose above her again and thrust into her, his eyes locked with hers, his soul needing to encompass the length and breadth and being of her with the same searing need that ruled his body. The world rocked in the colors of the sunset, soaring, shooting reds, golds that burned into heart and mind. He moved, and she moved with him, a fit as sweet as it was erotic. Fever seized him, and the rhythm of their union became staccato and desperate. The sounds of their breathing rose to storm pitch, hearts attuned in physical cacophony. Searing lava seemed to rip through his veins, and he fought it, until he felt her surge against him, and then his own climax seized him with violence and majesty.

He moved to her side, and felt the thundering in his chest decrease to a steady beat, the pulse slow, the air move. The colors of sunset faded. Mauve darkness settled over them as she curled against him. He touched her hair in wonder, but his voice rang harsh again when he spoke. "You can't go back there."

The wrong words. She pushed away from him.

"I have to."

"No."

"Jesse…"

"Shh."

"I have to go back. And I have to go back soon."

"Not now."

"They'll know I'm with you."

"It's early."

"But…"

"Shh."

"Jesse, you can work with me or against me," she whispered.

He didn't reply. He was fascinated by the color of her hair against his sheets in the dying light. She went rigid beside him, so he smoothed her hair, then her brow. Then he kissed her forehead, her lips.

And then it began all over again, and this time, when the final thunder came, the black of night had descended fully.

They didn't speak, just held each other for the longest time, her head on his chest, their legs entwined. At last she pushed away from him, rose and found the shower.

He found her there. And in the spray of heat and steam, he found himself exploring anew, touching, tasting, licking tiny water drops from her flesh….

Feeling them licked from his own skin, feeling himself touched, taken, stroked.

Soap upon flesh, flesh upon flesh, a night in which he found he could not be sated, in which he soared, in which he was afraid. And he didn't want it to end, because, when it did…

Eventually they managed an actual shower. The lights on, they moved in silence, finding all the scattered pieces of their clothing. And then, a new cup of coffee in his hand, Jesse told her firmly, "You can't go back."

She was rigid and determined; he could see that immediately. She regally smoothed back a piece of wet hair and said, "I told you, you can work with me and keep me safe, if that's what you feel you have to do. But I *am* going back."

"I can stop you," he told her.

She lifted her chin. "You'd really arrest me?" she demanded. "For what?"

His teeth grated.

"I can tell Harry that you're acting suspiciously. That I think you're dangerous." He lifted his hands in frustration. "Lorena, your being there is pure insanity. You've told me that someone killed your father. An innocent couple was shot down in cold blood. A man was eaten by a gator. If someone at Harry's is involved, that someone is ruthless."

She set her hands on her hips, indignant, eyes narrowing dangerously. "What? I'm a woman, and that means I have to be incompetent?"

"I didn't say that. But I'm not letting you go back there."

"Then you'll never find the killers you're after!" she told him.

He stared back at her, feeling anger rise in him again.

"I need to go back. And I need to go back now. I'm already going to have to think of something to say when everyone wants to know why you detained me."

"I told both you and Hugh that I was going to talk to you about the incident at the farm," he said flatly. He shook his head in disgust. "You're playing a dangerous game. You haven't just entered a pit of vipers, you're asking them to bite."

"What?"

"Oh, come on. You're flirting with the pack of them."

"I went for a ride in an airboat," she said. "So what?" But there was no conviction in her tone.

He stared at her, torn, impotent, and furious because he knew that, on the one hand, she was right.

He had no proof of anything. So…what? Wait until something else terrible happened and hope he was there to save her? Find some reason for a search warrant, a legal way to get into Harry's, and rip the place apart?

"No one was suspicious of me except you," she reminded him. "Honestly, Jesse, I told you I'm a crack shot. I carry a gun, and I'm licensed."

"Great. And do you walk around armed all day?"

She let out a sigh. "Do you really think anyone is going to hurt me in front of dozens of witnesses?"

"Two days," he said.

"What?" she asked him, frowning.

"Two more days. That's what I'll give you. And you have to swear to me that you'll go nowhere alone with any of those men. When it's night, you lock yourself in. When it's morning, you get where you need to be—fast."

"I need to get back into the lab," she said.

"You can do that when I'm there."

She cocked her head to the side, wary. "And we'll manage that how?"

"Easy. I'm around enough."

She hesitated. "Jesse—"

"That's the deal. Take it or leave it." He shook his head angrily. "You toe the line, and I mean it. It's going to be busy as hell right now, too, because I have to arrange hunting parties to find your scientifically mutated alligators—assuming they even exist. Every one of them has to be caught and killed. God knows how many people could die if some super race of huge, aggressive gators starts breeding out there."

"Two days, then," she said softly. "But, Jesse…that's my point, don't you see? I have to find the truth. I have to find out what they know and just how they've altered the alligators, not to mention just how many of them are out there."

"I need enough evidence to get a search warrant, nothing more," he said.

She nodded, then said softly, "I really have to go back now."

"I need a minute to get a few things," he told her.

"For what?"

"For the morning."

"You can't stay out there," she protested.

"Yes, I can."

"They'll know! Someone will definitely get suspicious if you start staying out there."

"No one is going to know."

"And how can that be?"

He smiled grimly. "Because you're going to sneak me into your room at night."

Her breath seemed to catch in her throat as she stared at him.

"Jesse, I've told you, I'm a crack shot."

"So was my wife," he informed her softly.

Then he turned away.

Chapter 8

Harry was beside the canal, looking both anxious and edgy, when they returned in the airboat.

Lorena cast Jesse a quick frown to warn him that they had clearly made the man suspicious.

"What are you two doing out this late at night?" he demanded.

Jesse managed to look a little sheepish as he tied up the airboat and helped Lorena to the embankment. She was surprised that he bothered, and that he could sound so casual as he said, "Just trying to avoid a problem."

"Maybe you want to let me in on it?" Harry said.

"We had a complaint, Harry," Jesse said. "But don't worry, it's all been nipped in the bud."

"What do you mean, don't worry? I thought I owned this place!"

"Just some kid said he'd been bitten by a hatchling.

Turns out, it was the kid's fault. He was trying to steal it," Jesse explained.

"Steal one of my hatchlings?" Harry looked enraged.

"Yep, and that's why the parents have dropped the whole thing. I just needed Lorena's account of the problem. There's nothing to worry about, Harry. I thought it would be a minor thing, and it was. If there had been anything to worry about, naturally I would have spoken with you immediately."

"This could mean a lawsuit," Harry protested.

"It might have, but it isn't going to," Jesse said.

Harry was still glowering. "It's my place. I need to be apprised of everything that happens here."

"Harry, chill. The complaint has been dropped. Lorena told me everything I needed to know. There was no reason to upset you."

Harry stared hard at Lorena. She tried to decide if he looked worried or not. Mostly he just seemed concerned about his place. And angry with Jesse. "You're not doing your job right, Jesse Crane," Harry said angrily. "Cutting corners, kidnapping my nurse."

Lorena was instantly aware that Harry had said the wrong thing. Jesse stiffened, and the look in his eyes turned chilling. "Harry, two good people have been shot to death, a tribal member has been killed by an alligator, and you've got a security guard in the hospital, hovering between life and death. Drop it," he said icily.

Harry backed down, instantly. "I, uh, I just checked on Roger. He's still in a coma," he said gruffly. "You found out anything else on the murders?" he asked.

"No," Jesse said simply. "Nor can I tell you anything else about Billy Ray. But we're going out gator-hunting from here tomorrow evening around six. The office will set things up with the guys who run the licensed hunts. I'll be needing Jack Pine and Hugh. We know we've got a man-eater out there, and it's got to be put down."

"Now you're going to take my handlers?" Harry said incredulously. "Like hell! This is a business."

"And you can do business tomorrow. You'll just be minus a couple of handlers come six o'clock."

"Dammit, Jesse—"

"How many tourists do you think you're going to have if this rogue gator attacks more people?" Jesse demanded.

Harry waved a dismissive hand. "Are you going to need my nurse again, too?" he demanded.

"Hopefully not," Jesse said calmly, not raising his own voice to meet Harry's indignant tone.

"You coming in for dinner?" Harry asked Jesse, clearly changing the subject to avoid an argument.

Jesse glanced at Lorena. "If there's still dinner, might as well," he murmured.

Harry made an unhappy snorting sound, and they walked together toward the main building. As they went, they could hear the bellowing of the alligators in their ponds.

Soon they reached the cafeteria. "I've eaten," Harry said curtly. "You two go on."

Lorena murmured, "Thank you," and stepped in ahead of Jesse.

Sally was seated at one of the tables, with Jack Pine and Hugh.

Hugh rose when he saw them enter.

"Well, that took a while," he said dryly.

"We got to talking, that's all," Jesse said.

Sally set a hand on his arm. "Jesse, how are you doing?" she asked, real concern in her voice.

Jesse frowned at her. "I'm worried," he said flatly.

Jack Pine waved a hand in the air. "Jesse, there may be one big gator out there, but face it, Billy Ray was a drunk. Do we really want to cause a panic out there when for all we know he passed out, fell in the water and drowned, and *then* got eaten by that gator?"

"No panic. Just a hunt," Jesse said.

"Let me get you all some food," Sally said sweetly, flashing a smile at Jesse, then Lorena. "It's late, they're closing down, so I'll just make sure you two get to eat."

"Thanks, Sally," Jesse said, smiling back at her.

Lorena found herself remembering how Sally had talked about Jesse earlier. *Devastated, but not dead!* She felt at a loss for a moment, realizing that she knew so little about him. The night had been strange. Intimacy had been sudden and yet…she felt as if it had been something that, unbeknownst to herself, she had actually been awaiting. But she didn't know anything about whatever might have gone on with him—and Sally?—before she got here. She did know that he'd had a wife, and that she was dead….

And that she'd been a crack shot.

"Harry teed off about the hunt?" Hugh asked.

Jesse shrugged.

"Harry's all about the bottom line," Jack said. "He doesn't even give a damn about Michael's research. He just wants to please the tourists, grow the gators, harvest the meat and hides."

"Yeah, but if we catch the rogue that killed Billy Ray, he'll want it on display, don't you think?" Sally said, returning to the table. One of waiters was behind her, carrying two plates piled with something Lorena couldn't identify.

"Jesse won't be letting Harry have that old gator, will you, Jess?" Jack said.

"Why not?" Harry asked.

"It should go to the village, to the Miccosukee," Jack said flatly.

"Let's catch the thing first," Jesse said.

"Hey…you're not going soft, are you? Thinking it's just a good ol' predator doing what comes naturally, and planning to transplant it somewhere deeper in the Glades?" Hugh asked.

Jesse shook his head. "No. It's dangerous. We have to put it down. There's one thing I'm really hoping, though."

"What's that?" Sally asked.

"That it *is* an 'it.' That we're not searching for more than one really dangerous alligator."

"There's one thing *I'm* wondering," Jack said.

"And what's that?" Lorena asked.

He stared at her. "Where the hell did a bugger that big and vicious come from?"

There was silence at the table. Lorena found herself intensely interested in her meal.

The conversation never really recovered after that.

Jack left the table first, a few minutes later. Then Hugh. Sally didn't seem to want to leave, though.

But finally Jesse stood. "Ladies, I've still got some work to do, so I'll bid you good night."

Sally watched him go, obviously appreciating the view.

Lorena cleared her throat. Sally glanced at her, her eyes sparkling with amusement. "Well, I see that you're coming to enjoy our local…wildlife, shall I say?"

Lorena ignored the other woman's teasing tone. "What happened to his wife?" she asked.

Sally didn't seem to mind dispensing information. "She was a cop, too. Some coked-up prostitute she was trying to help walked up to the back of her car one night and—on the order of her pimp—put a bullet into the back of her head."

Lorena let out a long breath. There was really nothing to say except "Oh."

"She was something, I'll tell you. An heiress determined to make the world better through law enforcement." Sally assessed Lorena carefully. "Don't go getting any ideas. He'll never marry again."

Lorena forced a smile. "Sally, I barely know the man."

"But you know enough, don't you?"

Lorena rose. "Like I said, I barely know the man. Thank you for making sure we could eat."

"He's interested in one thing, and one thing only. So you'd better play like a big girl, if you intend to play."

"Thanks for the advice," Lorena said lightly. "Good night."

As Lorena started walking away, Sally called softly after her, "Be careful."

Lorena spun back around. "Why?"

"Well, hell!" Sally laughed. "Old Billy Ray—eaten. And Roger... Just goes to show, you can never trust a gator. Believe me, I'm going to be very careful myself."

"Are you suggesting that Roger was helped into that pit?"

"Good God, no! He must have thought he heard something. Then leaned too far over the edge."

"So you think he fell in?" Lorena asked.

"Of course. Who would have pushed him?" Sally demanded.

"Hey, you're the one who warned *me*," Lorena said lightly, then smiled and left.

On her way to her room, she paused at the door to Michael Preston's lab and started to test the knob. Then she heard his voice from inside and stopped, listening. She thought maybe he was on the phone. His voice was low but intense.

She tried desperately to eavesdrop, but she couldn't make out his words. Nothing other than *giant* and *hunt*. There was nothing suspicious about that. By now everyone knew that Billy Ray had been killed by an alligator, a big one, and that it had to be hunted down and destroyed.

Still, she lingered, listening, until the sound of footsteps down the hallway warned her that she'd better get going. Worried that he might eventually have said something useful and now she was going to miss it, she gave up and hurried on to her own room.

Jesse took the airboat back to headquarters and checked in with his staff.

Brenda Hardy was there, doing paperwork. She perched on the edge of Jesse's desk. "I don't care what anyone says. There's more going on here than just some big gator. Billy Ray had a shotgun with him, he could shoot dead drunk. I'd bet cash money you're thinking what I'm thinking. All this happening at one time is too much to be coincidence."

Jesse nodded to her, then excused himself as his cell phone rang. It was Julie.

"Jesse."

"Julie. You all right?"

"Yeah…yeah. You know what I've been doing? Playing bingo out at the casino. I bought about a million cards. You can't think when you're trying to put little dots on a zillion numbers at once."

"Good, Julie. I'm glad. Anything that works for you is what you need to be doing."

"Right, I know. I had to tell you, Jesse. I drove out by the house before, and…and I drove back here as quickly as I could. I didn't go in. I didn't even get out of my car. But I saw the lights. I saw lights…like my mother said. I know why she thought aliens were landing. It was creepy…the way they seemed to come out of the swamp and the sky at the same time."

"Julie, don't go back there. Stay at the casino, stay in the bingo hall, at the machines, or locked in your room, all right? And don't tell anyone you drove by the house."

"All right, Jesse. I just thought you should know."

"I should, and I'm glad you called me. But you have to keep yourself safe. You understand?"

"I will, Jesse. I guess I thought I needed to go back to believe it. But I'll stay away."

"Promise?"

"I swear."

Jesse hung up. As he did, George Osceola walked over to his desk. Jesse looked up.

"You're not going to like this," George warned.

"What?"

"Dr. Thiessen, the vet, just called," George said.

"And?"

"He went back into his office tonight to get some notes. He'd decided to send the specimen and his samples to the FBI lab."

"And?"

When he got there, his night security man slash animal sitter was out cold in the kennel area."

"And let me guess. The alligator specimen and all the tissue and blood samples were gone?" Jesse said.

George nodded. "I'm meeting some of the fellows from the county out there now."

"I've got a drive to make," Jesse said. "Then I'll meet you there."

He got in his car and started speeding along the Trail, only slowing as he neared Julie's parents' house. He turned off his lights before he entered the drive, knowing that, even for him, that was foolhardy, considering the terrain.

He parked on the embankment that bordered the property. The crime tape still hung limply around the house itself and the place where Maria had died. The whole area seemed forlorn, desolate.

Whatever Julie had seen, Jesse realized after about twenty minutes of watching from the front seat, it was gone now. Tomorrow night, if Lars couldn't send a man to keep watch, he would send one of his own men, or even keep watch himself.

He got out of the car, carrying his large flashlight, and walked toward the water. As he reached the wet saw grass area that fell away from the hummock toward the water, he saw that the long razor-edged blades were pushed down. Once again, someone had been through with an airboat. He looked around but didn't see anything else suspicious.

When he got back to his car, he put a call through to Lars Garcia, despite the time. Lars already knew about the break-in at the vet's and was on his way out there.

When Jesse arrived at Doc Thiessen's, he found that the CSI team were already working, dusting for fingerprints, looking for footprints, searching for tire tracks, seeking any small piece of evidence.

Doc Thiessen had been born into a family of fruit-and-vegetable farmers in Homestead. He'd earned his veterinary degree at Florida State University and determined to come back to his own area to work. Now he had a head full of snow-white hair and a gentle, lined face. He worked with domestic as well as farm animals, and was known in several counties for his abilities to help with pet turtles, snakes, lizards, birds and commercial reptiles.

He was standing with Lars and the uniforms who had apparently been first on the scene when Jesse arrived. He shook his head as Jesse approached. "Jesse, I'm damned sorry. I was trying to prepare my samples properly, study them myself…I should have sent them straight out."

Jesse placed a hand on his shoulder. "It's not your fault. You couldn't have known this was going to happen. What about your night man? Jim? Did he see anything?"

"He's over there," Lars said, pointing. "Go on. I've already spoken with him."

Doc's night guard was a man named Jim Hidalgo, half Peruvian, half Miccosukee. He and Jesse were distantly related. They shook hands, and Jim looked at him, wincing. "Jesse, I didn't even see it coming. We've got a few dogs in the kennels, you know, belonging to folks on vacation. I heard something, went to check on the pups. One little beagle was going wild, and I walked over to it and…that's the last thing I remember until Doc was standing over me, taking my pulse."

"Thanks, Jim." The man had a bump the size of Kansas on the back of his head. Jesse stared at it and whistled softly. "You're lucky you're alive."

"They're insisting I go to the hospital," Jim said.

"Yeah, well…that's quite a bump. Let them keep an eye on you, at least overnight."

Jim sighed. "All right. If you say so."

Jesse walked back to Lars, who was waiting for him. He told him about Julie's call and his trip out to the house.

"I had officers out there last night," Lars said with a sigh. "It's just that the department only stretches so far. But I'll send some men out again, twenty-four-hour watch. Anything else? You find your rogue gator?"

"Not yet. We're doing an organized hunt tomorrow night." He hesitated. "We may be on to something, though."

"What?"

"I need someone else to explain it to you."

Lars's partner, Abe, walked up then. "You know something, Jesse? If so—"

"Know something? Let's see. A couple is murdered, and there's an alligator limb at the scene. A man is attacked and killed by an alligator. A guard falls or is pushed into an alligator pit, and now the vet's guard has been attacked and specimens have been stolen. Gee. Think anything might be related here? Does the word 'gator' mean anything to you?"

"Go to hell, Jesse," Abe snapped. "I want to know what you've got to go on. I'm Homicide. I look for human killers. You're the alligator wrestler."

"An alligator is a natural predator, Abe."

"My point. I can hardly arrest one."

"If an animal is trained to kill, that makes the trainer a murderer, doesn't it?" Jesse asked dryly.

"I just said that if you've got something—"

Jesse ignored Abe and turned to Lars. "How about lunch tomorrow? The Miccosukee restaurant? On me."

"Yeah, we can make it," Abe answered for Lars.

Jesse shook his head. "I have someone who may know something. But she won't talk if we make this too big a party. Abe, just let Lars handle it."

"Who is she?" Abe said angrily. "We can just bring her in."

"And do what? Issue a lot of threats and get nothing back?" Jesse asked angrily.

Lars set a hand on Abe's shoulder. "Partner, whatever I get, you know we share. So…"

Abe glared at Jesse. Jesse glared back. "Dammit, Abe, I'm not asking Lars to hide anything from you, and I'm not trying to hide anything myself. Hell, I'd invite anyone who could bring justice for Henry and Maria. But, Abe, you're not a guy with a gentle touch. Let Lars take this one. He can call you the minute he leaves."

"Fine," Abe grated.

With the crime-scene people busy at the vet's, Jesse knew there was nothing he could do there for the night. "I'm going to have a last word with Jim," Jesse said. "Lars, see you tomorrow."

They were almost ready to take Jim to the hospital for observation. He was being laid out on a stretcher.

"Jim?"

"Yeah, Jess?"

"You walked back to the beagle. You were hit on the head. Then nothing, nothing at all until Doc was there?"

"Nothing, Jesse. I'm sorry."

"That's all right."

"Does Doc usually come in at night?"

"No, but he'd been worrying about finishing up the work you wanted, 'cuz he hasn't been able to get to it during the day. We've been really busy lately. It's a bitch, huh?"

"Yeah, it's a bitch."

Then the med tech gave Jesse a thumbs up and rolled Jim into the vehicle.

Jesse waved and headed out.

Lorena should have been dog-tired, but she was nervous. Television couldn't hold her attention. She found herself prowling the room as the hour grew later.

He had said he would be here.

Irritated with herself, she sat down and tried staring at the television again. She thought she was just blanking on the screen, since she didn't understand a word that was being said.

Then she realized she was on a Spanish-language channel.

Insane.

She should work, she told herself.

Work, and not wonder if Jesse was really coming.

Work, and not feel on fire with such breathless anxiety, both physical and emotional….

What she'd told Sally was true: she barely knew the man.

It was also true that she needed to work. She hadn't managed much of her "real job" since she had come here. But then she had happened to arrive just when there had been terrible murders, and when a Native American who knew the canals better than his own features had met with his fate in those waters. There should have been time. Time to become trusted. Time to flirt, if necessary.

She needed to get into that lab.

She was convinced there were answers to be found there. She was usually so organized and analytical. But she was afraid to make notes, afraid that her room might be searched and her real purpose discovered.

She showered more to hear the sound of the water and feel the pounding of it against her flesh than anything else. Then she slipped into a cotton nightshirt and lay on her bed, but she still felt ridiculously keyed up.

Had he been serious. Was Jesse really coming back here? *Forget Jesse,* she told herself.

She tried to fathom the truth from what she had been able to glean from Michael's files. As yet, nothing that was proof positive. He was experimenting with gator eggs, of course. The temperature at which they were hatched determined the sex of an alligator; that kind of manipulation was easy. Breeding was basic biology. And here, at an alligator farm, it made sense to weed out characteristics one didn't like and fine-tune those features that were favorable to farming. Sex, size, the quality of the meat and hide.

But selective breeding hadn't created the monster she had seen today. Steriods and a formula—one that her father had known was too dangerous to exist—were behind what she had seen. Still, even if she got back into Preston's lab and found out what he was working on, how could she prove he had stolen her father's work?

Two days. Jesse had given her two days.

Just as she thought of the man, she heard a soft rapping at her door. She glanced at her glow-in-the-dark Mickey Mouse watch. It was after 1:00 a.m. She leapt from the bed, her heart thundering, and angry because of it.

The tapping sounded again. Then, softly, "Lorena, will you open the door?"

She hurried over, threw it open. "It's after one in the morning," she informed him.

He closed the door. "Shh."

"I actually do sleep at night. I have a job to do here. I wake up and start early. I—"

He drew her into his arms. "Shh."

"Jesse, I have to tell you—"

"Shh."

There was warmth in the depth of his eyes as well as amusement. There was something possessive in his hold, and she felt him slipping into her heart even as he inflamed her desires.

He's devastated, not dead. He'll never marry again. He's interested in one thing, and one thing only, so you'd better play like a big girl, if you intend to play.

He started to frown, staring into her eyes. "What's wrong? Has something happened?"

Lorena placed her fingers against his lips. "Shh," she said, and moved closer to him. His flesh was rich and warm, burnt copper, vibrant, vital.

He groaned softly, pulling her to him, and his lips found hers, pure fire. When they broke, she heard his whisper against her forehead, felt the power of his touch against her. "Lorena."

Fumbling, she found the light switch. And once again she said very softly, "Shh…"

Then she was in his arms. And the hour of the day or night didn't matter in the least.

When the alarm rang, rudely indicating that morning had come and it was time for the workday to begin, he was gone.

Chapter 9

It seemed to be business as usual at the alligator farm.

Lorena went through greeting the tourists and taking them to their first stop: Michael Preston's lab.

While working with a group of children, she tried to get a good look at the hatchlings and at the cracked eggs.

They appeared normal, as far as she could tell. She wished she had been more interested in her father's work at the time he'd been doing it, but she had simply never liked alligators.

It was the eyes, she was certain.

Two more groups of tourists came through. Michael was his usual self, valiantly trying to give a good speech, but obviously uncomfortable. Or maybe he only seemed so to Lorena because she knew he loved research and hated tourists. He did seem happy, however, to have her come through with the groups.

Happy to have her stay.

At eleven, her cell phone rang. It was Jesse. "I'm coming to get you for lunch," he told her.

"I'm not sure I'm supposed to leave during the day," she said.

"Everyone gets lunch. You won't even be ten miles away," he assured her.

At noon, he picked her up in front of the farm. He was in uniform. "Where are we going?" she asked.

He grinned. "A restaurant."

"Okay."

She had passed the place on her way out to Harry's she realized when they got there. It was directly across from the Miccosukee village.

Jesse glanced her way dryly. "Don't worry. You won't have to eat grilled gator or anything."

"I never thought I would," she responded. "You have a chip on your shoulder."

"I do not," he said indignantly, and she had to smile.

She balked when they reached the place and she saw that Lars Garcia was standing out front.

"What is this?" she demanded heatedly.

"You have to tell him what you think is going on."

"You gave me two days!" she said.

"There's been a complication. The vet's office was broken into. Another man was attacked. Thankfully, we have hard heads out here. He survived."

Jesse was grim, but she was still furious. She had nothing, no evidence at all, really, and he had brought her here to tell her story to another policeman. She was stiff and still angry when they went in.

Lars was as polite and decent as ever. He chatted about

the weather while they waited for their food, and he and Jesse talked about an upcoming musical festival put on by the Miccosukee tribe in the Glades. "People come by the hundreds. It's great," Lars said.

When their food came—she'd ordered a very boring meal: hamburger, fries and an iced tea—Lars lowered his voice and said, "Jesse says I need to know why you're here."

She'd thought she was tense already, but now her muscles constricted to an even greater degree, and she shot Jesse a furious glance.

"Lorena, it's important I know."

"Then I'm surprised Jesse didn't tell you," she said.

"I need to hear it from you."

She clenched her teeth, set her hamburger down, shot Jesse one last filthy stare, and explained what she knew and feared to Lars. He listened without mocking or doubting her, though he glanced at Jesse several times, as if Jesse might have put him in the middle of a science fiction tale, but when she finished, he sighed and asked, "Your father's death was ruled an accident?"

"Yes. But I know it wasn't."

"That's going to be very difficult to prove."

"Maybe not now, when other people are dying," she said.

That caused a glance between Lars and Jesse.

"What was in the e-mail from the alligator farm?" Lars asked.

She shrugged. "It was vague. They were interested, of course, in learning about any developments to increase quality and efficiency. They suggested that they could pay well."

"What was your father's reply?" Lars asked.

"That he had nothing ready as of yet. And he explained that research was difficult, that all genetic scientists had to take the greatest care when playing with the makeup of any life form."

"Did other alligator farms contact your father?" Lars asked.

She shrugged. "Yes."

"So why are you concentrating on this one?"

"Every other e-mail was signed by a specific person. At Harry's, the same e-mail account can be used by almost anyone who works there."

"We can trace the computer," Lars said.

"If so, what will that prove?" Lorena asked.

"Whether it was in the office, in the lab or somewhere else," Lars said.

"Preston would have to be involved, wouldn't he?" Jesse asked.

"There are no 'have-tos,' Jesse. We both know that," Lars said. He looked at Lorena. "You need to get out of that place."

She tensed again, staring at Jesse. "I can't see how I can be in any personal danger. I had nothing to do with my father's work."

"Anyone can be in danger," Lars said softly.

Lars sat back, wiped his mouth and stared at Lorena. "I'll have to talk to the D.A.'s office about a search warrant. In the meantime, you shouldn't go back."

Lorena leaned forward, speaking heatedly. "My father is dead. A local couple have been killed. You don't know how many enhanced alligators you might have running around the Everglades. You need me, and you need my help."

"There's something I don't understand here," Lars said, and he glanced at Jesse, frowning. "This research has to be fairly new. Alligators take time to mature and grow. How could this one have gotten so big so fast?"

Lorena shook her head. "The formula causes an increase in the growth rate. Take people. Better diets, rich in protein, make for taller, stronger teens. Body builders bulk up with steroids. You'd be amazed at what chemicals can do to the body. That's why it's so important not only that we find out who was doing what but to just how many specimens."

"We need a search warrant," Lars said simply.

"Do you think you can get one?" Lorena asked anxiously.

He shrugged. "If I can argue well enough. And prove just cause. Well, I should get moving." He lifted a hand to ask for the check. Jesse caught his arm.

"I told you yesterday. This one is on the tribe."

"Thanks." He rose. Lorena and Jesse did the same.

When Lars had walked out, Lorena turned on Jesse. "You told me that I had two days."

"Lorena, what do you think you're going to find in two days?" Jesse demanded.

"More than anyone else?"

"Is biochemistry another of your degrees?"

She gritted her teeth, staring at him. "No. But I know what might have been stolen from my father."

"Lorena, face it, you're not going to be able to do anything if you're dead!"

She turned away from him and headed toward the door, clearly indicating that lunch was over for her, as well.

He followed. As soon as he came out, she got into the car. There was no possibility that she was going to walk back to work.

He didn't pull straight back onto the road but instead drove almost directly across the street. She gazed at him with hostility. "You have a few minutes left. I thought you might want to see the village."

She didn't have a chance to refuse. He had already gotten out of the car.

They entered the gift shop first. It offered Indian goods from around the country. There were a number of the exquisite colorful shirts, skirts and jackets for which both the Seminoles and Miccosukees had become famous, along with dream catchers, posters, T-shirts, postcards, drums, hand-carved "totem" recorders and jewelry. Some of the unique beadwork designs on the jewelry might well have attracted Lorena's attention, but Jesse was already headed straight out the back. There was an entry fee, but Jesse just smiled at the girl, and he, with Lorena trailing behind him, walked on through. She offered the girl an awkward smile, as well.

Out back, there were a number of chickees, along with more items for sale. Women were there working on intricate basketry, sewing the beautiful colored clothing and designing jewelry.

Lorena, fascinated, would have paused, but Jesse was again moving on to one of the huge pits where alligators lived with a colony of turtles.

Looking into the pit, Lorena noted that a number of the gators were large, very large. But not one of them was more than ten feet.

"Jesse, what's up?"

A man with ink-dark hair and Native American features, wearing a T-shirt that advertised a popular rock band, walked up to them.

Jesse nodded to him. "Mike. This is Lorena Fortier. She's working at Harry's."

The man studied her with a smile. "Welcome."

"I thought she might want to see the village."

Mike smiled and shrugged. "Well, there's the museum, the pits, we do some wrestling, give a few history lessons."

"She's on lunch break. I just thought she should come look around. And I wanted to make sure you'd seen the notice."

"About the hunt tonight? I'll be there," Mike said grimly. He shook his head. "Billy Ray…well, he wasn't the kind of man that gave us a lot of pride, but hell, I wouldn't have wanted my worst enemy to go that way."

"Right. Make sure everyone knows we're hunting something big, really big. Close to twenty feet, maybe even more."

Mike whistled softly. "We do know what we're doing, Jesse," he said. "But it's good to be warned."

"See you later, then. And extend my thanks to everyone showing up from the tribe."

Mike nodded. "See you then."

Jesse turned and headed toward the exit without a word to Lorena. She had been angry, but now he was the one who seemed irritated. They reached the car, where, despite his apparent anger, he opened her door.

"You're the one who betrayed me," she reminded him.

He shot her a scowling glance. "I'm trying to get you out of what might be a dangerous situation. But you know what? I don't usually have a chip on my shoulder, but today, I do. Chemists, biochemists, biologists! They're playing with life. Interesting, sure. Let's see how we can improve what God made. But, the thing is, people play God, and things can happen. Billy Ray was no prize specimen of humanity. But you heard it in Mike's voice. He was one of ours. We're a small tribe. We were forced down to this land, and we learned how to live on it. Billy Ray had every right in the world to be fishing. Hell, if he wanted to drink himself silly, that was his choice, too. He shouldn't have been attacked by an animal that was only there because someone decided to play God."

Lorena gasped. "My father wanted to help people," she insisted angrily. "And when he was afraid he might be on to something dangerous, he was willing to destroy years of research!"

"Too bad you couldn't have explained that to Billy Ray while he was being eaten," Jesse said.

Lorena stared at him incredulously. "Evil people come in all colors and nationalities, you know!"

The drive from the village to the alligator farm was short. Jesse pulled in just as Lorena finished her tirade, and she was out the door before the engine could die. She walked around to his window. "Thank you for your concern for my safety, but since you've turned things over to Metro-Dade now, I'm sure I'll be just fine. You can feel secure in the fact that I'll be safe without your assistance."

She spun around, her feet crunching on the gravel path, heedless as to whether he called her back or not.

Lunch was over. It was time to get back to work.

She did so, energetically, talking to the tourists, helping Michael, even going with the tours to the pits and watching while Jack wrestled one of the six-foot alligators.

It didn't matter what she did, as long as she did something. With Michael in his lab, she certainly wasn't going to get anywhere there, so she put her heart into the business of people. Anything at all to keep busy.

To keep from thinking.

She shouldn't have gotten so close so fast. Getting intimate with someone so unique, so unusual, so very much…everything she might have wanted in life…had been more than foolhardy. She had let herself become far too emotionally involved, and then…

She'd felt that wretched knife in her back. His bitterness against her father had been unexpected and deeply painful.

That afternoon, she actually put her nursing skills to the test. A little girl fell on one of the paths.

Nothing like a registered nurse to apply disinfectant and a bandage.

As she tended the child, Lorena suddenly wondered why Harry had decided that he needed a nurse on the premises. It had made sense at first. The alligator farm was in an isolated location. But she had seen the local services in action. Help had arrived almost instantly when Roger had been found in the pit. Helicopters provided a swift transport to the emergency room.

Of course, nothing so drastic was necessary for little scrapes and bruises, but still…

Still, the question gave her pause. She forced herself to concentrate on it. It was good—no, it was *necessary*—to think about something—anything—other than Jesse Crane and the startling color of his eyes, the sleek bronze warmth of his flesh, the sound of his voice, the way he touched her, the structure of his face and the way she just wanted to be with him…

No! She had to think of something else.

He would be back at the end of the day, there to organize the hunt. As it veered toward five o'clock and closing, she determined to spend some quality time with Dr. Michael Preston.

* * *

By the time Lorena stalked off, Jesse had already cooled down and realized that he'd been a fool, taking his frustration over what had happened out on her.

What was it about the woman? She made him forget everything the moment he was with her, even though she wasn't his type at all.

And why not?

Because she was blond?

Elegant, feminine…a powder puff, or so he had assumed at first.

But she wasn't. She was determined. Reckless, maybe, but determined and fierce, and she had told him that she was a crack shot. Not a powder puff at all.

But also not the kind to spend a lifetime in the wilds. Then he reminded himself ruefully that his "wilds" were just a forty-five-minute drive from an urban Mecca with clubs, malls, theaters and more.

What was he doing, arguing with himself, convincing himself that his lifestyle was a good one? Because…?

Because he hadn't felt the way he felt about her in a very long time. In fact, he'd thought he'd buried those feelings along with Connie, that as long as he threw himself back into his passion for the land and the tribe, he could learn to live without all they had shared, the tenderness and sense of being one, loving, laughing, waking together, sleeping each night entwined. There was the chemistry that brought people together, and, if you were lucky, the chemistry, excitement and hunger that remained. And more. The longing to see someone's eyes opening to the new day, the times when no words were necessary, the nights when life was good just because the world could be shared.

He lowered his head, wincing, feeling as if the scars that had covered his wounds were ripping open. As if they were raw and bleeding, all because of the promise of something, some*one,* else. But that promise brought with it the one emotion he dreaded more than anything. Fear. No wonder he'd pushed her away.

He clenched and unclenched his fists. This wasn't the right time. In fact, it was idiotic. And, anyway, she was furious with him, probably regretting the very fact that they'd touched.

He forced his mind onto the case.

He felt that they were closing in, that Lars would be able to get the search warrant after what he had learned from Lorena. There were, however, other alligator farms in the area. It might be tough for him to convince the D.A.'s office, without concrete proof, not only that there really were "enhanced" alligators in the Everglades, but that Harry's Alligator Farm and Museum was responsible, and that whoever had gone to the extremes of biochemical manipulation was also willing to kill for it.

He hesitated, then decided to take another drive out to Dr. Thiessen's place to see if the Metro-Dade cops had missed anything, though he doubted it. They were good.

Then again, this was a world he knew far better than anyone else, a world that could not be taught in any lab or classroom.

In her room, Lorena found herself amazed to be carefully considering her wardrobe for the evening.

She hadn't been asked on the hunt, which made sense. Only experienced alligator trappers were going, and that definitely did not include her.

Nor, she suspected, did it include Michael Preston.

Which was good, because she wanted to spend some time with Michael. She didn't want to appear as if she had dressed to seduce, but she *did* want to look attractive.

Not in an aggressive way. Just enough to be compelling, so she could conduct her own hunt this evening.

She opted for casual slacks and a soft silk halter top. When she was dressed, she headed for his lab, listened, and heard movement. She tapped on the door.

"Yes?"

Lorena slipped in. "Hey. Are you going on that hunt this evening?" she asked him.

He arched a brow, grimaced and shook his head. "I'm a scientist. The brains, not the brawn."

"Ah."

"I guess you're into brawn."

"I am?"

"Well…" He perched on the edge of his desk, still in his lab coat. "You've been spending a lot time with our bronzed-and-buff policeman, Ms. Fortier."

She shrugged casually. "Not really. I wound up driving with him when that poor woman freaked out over her friend having been killed. And I probably shouldn't have headed out to the casino to begin with, the night I left with him. Too tired. And then someone told him about the incident with the hatchlings, so he wanted to talk to me."

"Not me."

"Did you tell anyone here?" Lorena asked.

He lifted his shoulders. "I don't think so. Maybe the kid complained in the end, I don't know. Maybe we shouldn't have let the little brat off the hook."

"Maybe not," she agreed. She walked closer, then sat on

the other corner of his desk. She frowned. "Michael, did you ever believe any of those stories about kids buying baby alligators and then their parents flushing them down the toilet, so they wound up in the sewers of New York, that kind of thing?"

He waved a hand in the air. "Science fiction," he assured her.

"Alligators, even in a sewer, wouldn't last long in New York. They need the sun, the heat. You know that."

"Right," she mused. "But…down here, I wonder how many alligators wind up free after they've been lifted from a place like this one by a kid like that brat. I mean it's possible. We both know that."

He slipped from his position on the desk and approached her, a smile on his face. She was a bit unnerved when he came very close, leaning toward her, resting his hands on the desktop on either side of her. "Possible," he said softly, his face just a whisper away. "But no kid is going to steal a hatchling from here, then let it loose in the New York sewers to grow into a monster."

"But there's at least one monster alligator out in the canals right now," she said. "That's what they're hunting tonight."

She saw a pulse ticking in his cheek. He didn't move. "Just what are you suggesting, Ms. Fortier?" he asked very softly.

"What else could it be?" she asked innocently. "I think that alligator escaped or was stolen from a lab," she said, and shrugged.

"From here?" he asked.

"From somewhere," she breathed. He was close. So close. And he might be the brains and not the brawn, but he still had quite an impressive build, and she just might have taken things too far.

"If I could create a super-gator, I'd be rich," he said, sounding surprisingly disgusted.

But she could see the tension in his face, feel it in his muscles. Her recklessness could prove dangerous. This, however, had been the time to take chances. Dozens of men from around the area would be arriving shortly. If he came any closer...

If she felt a deeper surge of unease...

All she had to do was scream.

He was staring at her intently. Searching her eyes.

He started to raise a hand toward her face, smiling.

"Michael?"

The call and a fierce knocking were followed by the door simply opening.

Lorena slipped from the edge of the desk as Michael turned.

Harry was there.

"Michael, can you get out here and help with the equipment? This is insane, if you ask me. Half the guys have no supplies. Damn Jesse. Leave it to him to get the full cooperation of the Florida Wildlife and Game Commission for a wild-goose chase."

If Harry had noticed that he had interrupted something, he gave no sign. But maybe he hadn't noticed, she thought. He seemed much more upset about the hunt than that a man had been killed by a gator.

Lorena grimaced as she caught Michael's eye, then escaped in Harry's wake.

Hurrying out back to the canal, she saw an unbelievable lineup of airboats and canoes. Jesse was up on some kind of a huge tackle box, giving instructions. "Remember, folks, we're looking for something really large—not indiscriminately killing off a population for trophies."

"How big, Jesse?" a man shouted from one of the canoes.

"Bigger than the norm," Michael Preston answered for him, hurrying forward. "The biggest gator ever recorded in Florida was seventeen feet, five inches long. The biggest gator recorded in Louisiana was nineteen feet, two inches. So if you find anything smaller than that—wrong gator."

"Ah, hell!" the same fellow snorted. "We have to have something real to go by."

"You heard the man. We're looking for fifteen feet or over. All right?" Jesse asked.

"We get to harvest what we get?"

She saw Jesse defer to a man who looked like he was about to go on safari, in khakis and a straw hat. He was tall and lean.

Jesse reached a hand down and helped the man up on the box. "This is Steven Bear, Florida Wildlife and Game Commission."

"We can harvest the fellas, huh?" another man called.

"Gentlemen, the important thing is this—we're not out on a regular hunt. Make sure your quarry is over fifteen feet. Then the meat is yours. Nothing small is to be taken. Understood?"

She saw both Steven Bear and Jesse jump down from the box. Someone asked Jesse a question, and he answered, then headed for an airboat with a number of men already aboard.

Michael came up behind her. "Half those guys see this as a free-for-all," he murmured.

She turned to him, frowning herself. "I don't get it. I

mean, there are so many boats. Are they going to try to sneak up on it with all those lights, all that noise?"

"You'll see," Michael said.

And she did. It had seemed like chaos, but when the airboats took off, they headed in all different directions. Once again, she had forgotten that what appeared like solid ground in this area most often wasn't.

River of grass.

They were taking off over that river in a dozen different directions.

"Well, they'll be gone awhile," Michael said. "Why don't we have some dinner?"

"Sure."

They ambled to the cafeteria together, chose pork chops for their meals, and sat together.

The place was almost eerily empty. "Did Sally go on the hunt?" Lorena asked, curious that the outspoken, sexy redhead was nowhere to be seen.

"I didn't see her," Michael said.

"Does she help with the research here at all?" Lorena asked.

Michael laughed. "There's only one green thing that Sally would research—money," he told her.

"Oh?"

"Um."

Lorena smiled, smoothing back a lock of hair. "I don't get it then. Why is she working out here?"

"I think she's trying to be so indispensable to Harry that he makes her a partner. He owns land all over the place. And we're doing well here…but I think he'd like to open another facility, closer down by the Keys. He's already opened a few shops in Key Largo."

She frowned again. "Michael, this is a totally dumb

question. But Harry raises gators for their meat and hides, right? So where does he—"

"Lorena!" Michael said, grinning. "You don't 'harvest' animals where you show them off to the tourists! I told you—Harry owns a lot of land closer to the Keys, down in the Florida City–Homestead area."

"Ah."

"You really are interested, aren't you?" When she nodded, he said, "I can show you a few things, then. Are you done?"

"Um, yes," she murmured.

He wiggled his eyebrows in a manner suggestive of a hunched Igor in a horror movie. "Come, my dear, I'll show you my lab," he growled jokingly.

Lorena froze for a moment. She'd been doing everything in her power to sneak into the lab, and now he was making this offer.

While anyone who might have come to her rescue was off hunting for a rogue alligator.

No. There were more live-ins around the compound. And Harry hadn't gone on the hunt; he was around somewhere.

Besides, she had waited far too long for this opportunity. She could take care of herself.

And she was going in.

"Let's see what you've got to show me," she said with a smile.

He flashed her a smile in return, showing very white teeth. They rose and walked across the compound. She noted that there was another guard on duty.

She noted as well that he was spooked. When he heard their footsteps, his hand flew to the hilt of his gun, buckled at his hip.

"Just Ms. Fortier and me," Michael said.

"Evenin'," the guard replied.

When they reached the door to the lab, Michael drew out his keys and opened it, pressing the small of Lorena's back lightly to get her to proceed inside.

He followed, closed the door, then locked it.

Then he turned and stared at her. "I don't know why I bother. Someone picked it open the other day."

"Oh?"

He shook his head, approaching her. She cocked her head, looking at him. The guard had just seen the two of them together. He couldn't possibly be planning anything…evil.

Not unless he meant to go back out and kill the guard as well!

He was still smiling, as if his intent was to seduce, but she knew it wasn't. She found herself backed against the desk.

He was the brain, he had said, not the brawn. But he was a liar. She could feel the heat and strength of his muscles.

And his anger.

His menace…

"You picked the lock, Lorena, didn't you?" he asked softly.

"What?"

"Ah, the innocence. Like hell, Ms. Fortier. You're flirting madly with me, while it's more than obvious that it's Jesse Crane who's really stirred your senses. And yet you're charming as hell to Jack and Hugh, too. Are you just a little vamp, Ms. Fortier? I don't think so. I think you're up to something. You want something in this lab. Tell me what it is. Here we are, you and me, alone, finally. So…it's time. You want to see what's going on in here? You might as well. I think you should see exactly what you've been wanting to see. Now. *Right now.*"

Chapter 10

Nighttime in the Everglades, and it was eerie.

No matter how well a man knew the place, the near-total darkness hid the predators haunting the swamp and made this a dangerous place.

When light touched the gators' eyes, they glowed, as if they were demons from hell, not of this world at all.

Jesse was accustomed to the glowing eyes, and yet even he found them chilling in the dark of the night.

Despite his familiarity with the creatures, it was difficult for him to determine the size of one with only the eyes to go on. Sometimes, he knew instantly when he was looking at an animal of no more than five to eight feet, but with just the eyes above the water to go by, more often than not it was a crap shoot.

Twice they snared a creature only to realize that the

specimen they had in their loops was no more than nine feet, ten tops.

Each time they released their catch. Enraged, the alligators made swift departures from the area once they had been freed.

The rest of the group on the airboat, Jack, Leo and Sam Tiger, were soaked and exasperated, but no one suggested giving up as they moved closer to the location where Billy Ray had been attacked and killed.

They had been out a few hours and had just cut the motor, and only the noises of the night were echoing in the air around them, when Jack Pine said softly, "There," and pointed.

Jesse looked in the direction Jack was indicating.

The alligator wasn't completely submerged. The length of the head was incredible. He focused hard and saw the length of the animal as it floated just beneath the surface.

And he knew they had found the beast they were searching for.

Sam whistled softly. "I have never seen anything remotely near that size before," he said.

"Let's bait it," Jesse murmured.

Their bait was chicken. He tied several pieces on the line.

The alligator watched them as they approached. It didn't move; it showed no fear.

When the line was cast in the water, the animal moved at last.

It went for the bait. They were ready with their snares.

A massive snap of the mighty jaws severed the lines as well as securing the meat, but Jack managed to get a noose around the neck.

The alligator made one swing of that massive head.

Jack went flying off the airboat, a shout of surprise escaping his lips. The animal instantly began to close in on him.

Sam quickly started the engine and headed in for a rescue. Jesse went for one of the high-powered revolvers. He aimed and fired, aimed and fired, as they neared Jack.

Sam swore, shouting to Jack.

In a frenzy, Jack moved toward the airboat.

Jesse, taking care to miss the man, fired again and again.

Ten bullets into the gator.

It kept coming, heedless of the men, heedless of the bullets that had pierced its hide.

They reached Jack. Sam and Leo instantly reached for him, and he reached back, grabbing their hands, the muscles bulging in his forearms and a look of dread in his eyes.

They were just dragging Jack over the edge of the airboat platform when the gator's head emerged, mammoth jaws wide with their shocking power.

Jesse aimed again, dead into one of the eyes.

The explosion ripped through the night.

The eye and part of the head evaporated.

And at last, with Jack's feet just clearing the water, the creature began to fall back.

Jesse fired again and again, aiming at what was left of the disappearing head.

He felt a hand on his arm. Sam's. "You got it," Sam said softly.

And from where he lay on the floor of the airboat, Jack said softly, "Dear God."

In the silence that followed his statement, they heard the whir of motors, saw approaching lights and heard the shouts of others.

More airboats and canoes arrived, and the area was suddenly aglow with floodlights.

"You got it?" Hugh called from another vessel.

Jesse realized that he was shaking. He nodded, turned, lowered his gun and found a seat.

The others began to haul the creature in.

"Well, Lorena?" Michael asked huskily.

Great, she thought.

She had a gun, and she was a crack shot. But she had let her eagerness to find the truth lead to stupidity, so here she was, boxed in by her main suspect, and he was challenging her....

She slid her hands backward on his desk. In all the old movies, there was a letter opener on a desk, ready to be used by a desperate victim as a weapon.

There was nothing on Michael Preston's desk but his computer and a few papers.

Not even a paperweight.

"Well..." she murmured, as he came closer. Closer.

There was nothing of use on the desk.

She told herself to scream!

It was all she had left.

"How could you?" Michael said suddenly, turning abruptly away from her.

She gulped down her scream.

"What?"

"How in the world could you suspect me of anything? Although what you think I've been doing, I still don't know. You've been on my computer. You've been searching this lab. What do you think that I've done? Or are *you* out to steal something from *me?*" he demanded.

She stared at him, a frown furrowing her brow. He seemed to be genuinely upset, and he also seemed to be as much at a loss as she was herself right now.

But if not Michael Preston…who? He was the scientist here.

The brains, not the brawn.

"What?" she repeated, stalling for time, rapidly trying to determine just what to say.

"Are you a thief?" he queried.

"Of course not!" she protested.

"Then what have you been doing?"

She sighed, looking downward. "Trying to understand," she murmured.

"Understand what?" he demanded.

"Well, you know, more of what's going on around here."

"Really. Didn't the concept of simply asking occur to you?"

Again she sighed. "Well…no. It's all so strange. This place, the people here."

"Except for Jesse Crane."

She stared at him, then shrugged. "He seems to be a decent guy. I like him," she murmured.

"In a way you don't like me?"

"Oh, Michael! You're great. You know that. Half the women you meet immediately start crushing on you," she told him.

He grinned ruefully, then shrugged. "The problem is," he said huskily, "it's the half of the female population I *want* that couldn't care less about me."

Lorena felt awkward then, not sure what to say. But feeling awkward was much better than feeling terrified.

"Michael…"

"Never mind. It's true. Women prefer brawn to brain."

She arched a brow. "Are you insinuating that men with brawn can't have brains? I have the impression that you spend a fair amount of time in the gym."

He sat beside her on the desk, crossing his arms over his chest. He sounded amused as he admitted, "Yeah, I go to the gym. But do I want to be out looking for a giant gator? Not in this lifetime. I like hatchlings. They're little. They might bite fingers, but it's unlikely that I'll become dinner for them."

"Michael…have you ever altered a hatchling?"

"Altered?"

"When you crack the eggs. Have you ever experimented?"

"Yes," he said flatly. His eyes narrowed sharply as he stared at her. "Is that what you're after? Trying to steal my vitamin compounds?"

"Vitamins? No."

"Well, that's about all I've worked with. Vitamins in the egg. You want my password? You want to get into the files you haven't been able to crack?" he asked.

She was uneasy again, thinking that he might have refrained from harming her only because he hadn't decided what she was really doing, why she had come.

Was this a trap?

"Just what kind of work are you doing?" she inquired.

"What do you think?" he demanded. "The same kind of research as everyone else! Alligator meat is already lean and high in protein. I'm trying to make it even better, so someday it can feed the world."

He sounded like her father. But she wondered if he was driven by the same true passion to help, or if he was seeking renown—or just money.

He shook his head with disgust suddenly and walked around to click on his computer. "What kind of work do I do? Research, and yes, experimentation. But you know what? Nothing I know about can create a giant killer gator. So you go ahead and take a look. I hope you're up on your enzymes, proteins, compounds, vitamins and minerals."

"Look, Michael," she began. "I—"

He was typing something when he suddenly looked up. "I just realized something. Why are you looking into *my* research? For a gator to have gotten as big as this one supposedly is, it would have to have been growing for years and years—while both of us were still kids, practically."

"Not that long," she murmured dryly.

He stared at her, then exhaled slowly. "Is there some kind of research out there that I don't know about? Some kind of discovery. That is…what you're saying is impossible."

"Hey," she murmured, keeping her eyes low. "I'm not a researcher. I'm not even an alligator expert."

"So what are you after?"

"I'm not sure. I'm just curious, I guess," she lied. She still wasn't certain she could trust Michael Preston.

He shook his head, studying the computer screen. "There have been big gators, but the biggest one on record wasn't even caught in this state. I suppose someone could have figured out a way to jump-start gator growth, or hybridize a gator with something else. I mean, we only have beefalo because of somebody's bright idea to breed a cow with a buffalo."

He seemed genuinely absorbed in seeking answers, but Lorena found that she was uncomfortable despite that fact.

"Come. Look," he demanded, staring at her belligerently.

She walked over to see the screen. He stood, urging her into the chair.

He had opened his research files. He had been telling her the truth—at least, as far as this proved. There were notes on the eggs with cracked shells. There was a study on albino alligators, with statistics regarding their life expectancy in the wild. There were side notes reminding him to speak to Harry about habitat changes, notations regarding the fact that he intended to set the temperature to create a male so they could eventually breed it with a number of females and track its genetic influence.

As she read his notes, she could feel him. He was standing directly behind her chair.

"Go on," he snapped, sounding angry again. "Keep reading."

Words began to swim before her eyes. She wondered how much time had passed.

It felt like forever.

She pushed the chair away from the desk, pushing him back, as well. "Michael, I told you, I'm not a researcher, so I don't even understand what I'm reading. I was just curious." She stood. "And I'm tired, really tired."

He shook his head. "You're not leaving here. Not until you tell me what you're up to."

"I'm not up to anything," she lied flatly.

"Then why break into my lab?"

She lowered her head, seeking a plausible explanation. She looked up at him again, knowing she had to be careful. "Michael…you're an attractive man."

"So?"

"I…well, frankly, I was interested in you. As a man. As a scientist. I was curious about you. I wanted to know what made you tick, why you're so fascinated with such strange creatures. But then…"

"Then you met Jesse."

She shrugged, not wanting to commit.

"You're sleeping with him," he accused her.

"Michael, that's really none of your business."

"Ah, I see. You break into my lab because of a crush on me—sorry, interest in my life, what makes me tick—but *your* life is none of my business."

She lifted her hands. "I'm sorry."

"I should report you to Harry."

"Do whatever you feel you have to," she murmured, looking down.

"You're making a mistake, you know."

He was close to her again. Just a foot away.

He reached out a hand. She nearly jumped.

He touched her face. "A big mistake," he told her.

"I'm afraid I've already made more than a few of those in my life," she murmured.

He tilted her chin upward, meeting her eyes earnestly. "No. You're making a big mistake with Jesse. You don't even know him."

"I know something about his past, if that's what you mean," she said.

"He's a loner, Lorena. Do you want to spend your entire life sitting on a mucky pile of saw grass? He belongs here. You don't. His passion is the land and the tribal council. He's decent enough as a human being. But he puts a wall up. He always will. Think about it."

She caught his hand and squeezed it. Like a friend. She was more anxious than ever to get the hell out of his lab.

"Michael, we've got a bigger problem than my love life right now. There's a killer gator out there."

"People have been killed by alligators before," he said flatly.

"Yes, but this is different. And we breed gators here. People are liable to think we have something to do with it."

He laughed a little bitterly. "You think? Who cares? Maybe that gator will make things better here. Think about it. People love to stop and stare at accidents. They love horror movies. People don't mind watching terrible things happen to strangers. I think the fact that there's a man-eater out there will draw even bigger crowds."

"Michael, that's horrible!"

He shrugged. "A lot that's horrible is true."

She hesitated for a moment, feeling another tremendous surge of unease.

"They should be coming back soon," she murmured. "Very soon."

"Are you trying to get away from me?" he asked her.

She straightened determinedly. "I want to see if they're back yet, if they've caught that thing," she said.

She headed for the door.

She felt him following her.

For a minute she was terrified that she wouldn't be able to open the door easily, since it was locked.

She twisted the knob, feeling his heat as he moved up close behind her, almost touching her.

She was certain he was reaching out, about to grab her, but the door opened easily, and as she threw it open, Sally was coming down the hallway.

"Sally!" she exclaimed loudly.

If Michael had been about to touch her, his hand fell away. "Hey, Sally."

"I think they're coming back," Sally was saying excitedly. "Harry was just on the radio with someone. They've got something."

"They caught it?" Michael asked.

"Well, I don't know if they caught 'it,' but they caught something. Come on."

Jesse felt drained and uneasy when they arrived back at Harry's. Jack Pine had come too damn close to being that alligator's last meal.

But he was apparently the only one who felt uneasy. Everyone else, including the hunters who had come back empty-handed, seemed to be on some kind of a natural high—amazed and excited by the size of the creature.

"It's a record," Harry said as the men made their way to land, a number of them dragging the nearly headless carcass onto the hard ground.

Harry was barking out orders, getting people to take measurements. He, too, seemed pleased and excited.

Jack, who had been given the tape measure, cried out, "Son of a gun, we just beat Louisiana. Twenty-two feet, three inches!"

"I don't care what it costs, we need the best taxidermist in the country. What's left of this sucker is getting stuffed. Hell, who shot the thing so many times? Never mind, never mind, the bullet holes are good. They make him look tougher than a *Tyrannosaurus rex*," Harry said.

"Harry, it's going to a lab. There's going to be an autopsy," Jesse said. He was drenched and covered in muck, and in no mood for the spirit of joviality going around. The thing had been a killer.

"An autopsy? On a gator?" Harry said.

Jesse felt his stomach turn. "We need to know for sure if this was the animal that took down Billy Ray."

Silence fell over the crowd at last as they all realized what Jesse was saying.

The gator would still have been digesting its last meal when it was killed.

"All right, Jesse. Have it taken to the lab." Harry sounded unhappy but resigned. "Do I get it when you're done?"

Jesse didn't answer, just turned away. Lorena was there, standing back in silence.

He felt a flip-flop of emotion.

In the heat of the hunt, he'd forgotten that he'd left her here. Alone.

But she appeared to be fine. More than fine. As ever, she was stunning. A rose in the midst of swamp grass.

"Are you taking the carcass to Doc Thiessen?" Harry asked.

Jesse kept staring at Lorena as he answered. "They'll have better facilities upstate, at the college," he said, turning away from Lorena at last.

Everyone had their cameras out now. They had hoisted the alligator up over one of the steel light poles. The thing was actually bending with the weight. Everyone had gone back to talking excitedly and having their pictures taken with the carcass.

The head…just the head…dear lord. The size of what was left was terrifying.

Lorena stayed apart from the crowd, but he saw that Michael and Sally were posing, Hugh snapping the picture.

"Harry, we'll see about getting the gator to you when we're done, okay?" he said congenially.

"Folks, we got the cafeteria open!" Harry called out, beaming at Jesse's words. "There's just coffee and sandwiches, but you're all welcome!"

Still grinning broadly at Jesse, Harry walked away.

Lorena was still a good twenty feet away, but her eyes were on him.

"Hey," he said softly.

"Hey." She smiled, apparently having forgiven him, and walked toward him slowly.

Damn, but he was in love with just the way she walked. The slow, easy sway of her hips. The slight look of something secretive, something shared, in the small curl of her lips. The way her hair picked up the lights, burning gold.

She reached him and touched his face, apparently heedless as to whether anyone noticed or not.

"You know, Officer Crane, you look good even in muck," she told him.

"I'd be happy to share my muck," he told her.

"Not here," she whispered. He thought she shivered slightly. "Not tonight."

"Are you coming home with me, then?"

Her head lowered; then she looked up, and her smile deepened. "Yeah, yeah, I guess I am."

The feeling of dread and weariness that had taken such a grip on him as they returned seemed to melt away. Strange, how life could be, how human emotions could be changed by something as simple as the sound of someone's voice.

The sway of someone's hips. Her smile.

Chemistry. She had been fascinating but unknown, and

now she was known. Everything he knew now made her slightest movement all the more seductive. The thought of touching her again was deep, rich, combustible.

"Should we take my car?" she asked.

He arched a brow with a rueful smile, indicating the state he was in.

"I told you, I like you in muck."

"Down and dirty, eh?" he teased.

"I was thinking of a shower," she murmured.

"Jesse!" someone called excitedly.

He was startled from the absorption that had made him forget that dozens of people surrounded them.

"Jesse!" It was Sally. She came over and gave him a big hug. "Aren't you excited? That's the biggest gator on record, and you're the one who bagged it."

"It was a killer, Sally."

"That makes you one big, bad hunter, then, doesn't it?"

There was innuendo in her voice. Once it had amused him, but now it was an imposition.

She suddenly realized she had her back to Lorena and turned. "Oh, I'm sorry, Lorena. It's just so exciting."

Exciting? Yeah, Sally was excited, Jesse thought. Sally was the kind who found sensual stimulation in danger.

He looked at Lorena, and at that moment he realized that he was falling in love. She was clearly amused by the situation. Her eyes didn't fill with anger, fear or suspicion; there was even a slight smile on her face. She was willing to let him handle it. And she would wait.

"It was an alligator, Sally. Thousands of alligators are killed on hunts. But I guess you're right. There are people who like the hunt. Frankly, I'm not a hunter."

"Jesse! Your people have lived off gators for over a century, hunting them, wrestling them."

For some reason, the way she said "your people" didn't sit right with him. He realized suddenly that Sally would always be fascinated with someone for what they did, not who they were. He hadn't really given it any thought before, but she'd never been more than someone with whom to enjoy a friendly flirtation. Tonight, he found that he was slightly repelled.

A wry smile came to his lips. That was, of course, because he'd never realized he could actually fall in love with anyone again.

"Isn't the casino the big moneymaker these days?" Lorena asked, her smile growing deeper as she and Jesse met each another's eyes.

"Oh, yeah. Bingo," Jesse agreed. "But we're all glad this guy's been caught. I think he's the one that got Billy Ray, and we'll know for certain soon enough. Good night, Sally."

He didn't actually step around her, just eased into a position that let him slip an arm around Lorena's shoulders.

"Good night, Sally," Lorena said.

The woman stared blankly at the two of them for a moment. Then she seemed to realize that they were leaving. Together.

"Oh! Uh, good night."

They avoided the cafeteria, where people had started massing. As they walked down the hallway, they could hear Jack talking. "I'm telling you, I thought I was a goner. If it hadn't been for Jesse, I'd have been chum."

Outside, Jesse protested again. "Lorena, this is swamp muck. Heavy, smelly dirt. The car—"

"There's a towel in back. You can throw it over the seat," she said. After rummaging for a moment, she found the towel and put it over the driver's seat.

"Hey, I'm the dirty one," he told her.

"And I don't know where I'm going. You need to drive."

She tossed him the keys. He shrugged. It was true. If you didn't know where to take an almost invisible road off the Trail, you were never going to find his house.

It was no more than a ten-minute drive, and both of them were too preoccupied to talk. And they were barely inside the door before she had slid into his arms, shivering slightly, clinging to him, her arms slipping around his neck, her body pressed to his, her lips seeking his mouth. It seemed an eon of ecstasy that they remained thus, and he felt a renewed sense not just of fervor and hunger, but of that deeper rise of emotion that came from the fact that they had made the subtle adjustment from wanting to needing, from carnal chemistry to a melding of body, heart and soul. She, too, was soon covered in swamp mud, and they made their way to the bathroom, where he managed to turn on the shower spray while disrobing himself and her, barely breaking contact the whole time.

Flesh, naked flesh, soap and suds, and hands. She touched him everywhere. He returned the favor. She had magic hands, taking a slow course of discovery. Light on his shoulders at first, and then with a pressure that both alleviated strain and created the sweetest strain of a very different kind.

Her fingers played down the length of his spine, over his hips. He touched her in return. The darkness of his hands over the pale roundness of her breasts was arousing, his palms rubbing over her nipples before his head ducked and his mouth caressed them. The water sluiced through her hair. He caught it and cast it over her shoulder, turning her against him so that his lips could fall on her nape, below her ear, on her shoulders, her back. He turned her in his arms, continuing his erotic ministrations against her abdomen, her thighs, then between them. She gripped his shoulders, quivered at his touch, moaned slightly, then cried out, sliding down in sudsy sleekness to meet his mouth with the furious hunger of her own once again.

Her hands were delicate, then fierce, stroking against his chest. They knelt together in a steaming spray that seemed almost fantasy, something keener, sharper, than he'd ever known before. She stroked his sex with her hands and tongue, and he wound his arms around her, bringing them both to their feet, bracing her against the tile of the shower, lifting her until she came back down on him and the hard arousal of his sex slid easily into her. He nearly whispered the words to her then, that he was more than physically one with her, that he was falling in love. But he would never have her doubt such words, as she would if they were spoken in the urgent desperation of the desire that drummed through him like a storm tearing the Glades asunder, so he whispered instead that she was beautiful, and the words she returned were ever more arousing. He became aware of the ancient thunder throbbing through his body, his lungs and his heart, and in a matter of moments they climaxed together in the steamy spray. The winds began to ease while they remained entwined.

Later, when they had sudsed again, then slipped into each other's arms to sleep, but wound up making love again, he held her, spooned against him. He lay awake, stroking her hair, in wonder. He had thought he would never find a woman like his wife again, someone who had loved him fiercely, been brave and funny, sweet and strong, an equal, but able to make him feel his own strengths, that he was very much a man.

And, of course, he hadn't found his wife again. In a place in his heart, he would love and cherish her forever.

He had found someone unique, who was passionate and righteous, confident, her own self. Different, and yet with qualities that resonated in his heart and soul.

He adjusted his position slightly. Pressed his lips to the top of her head. "I think I'm falling in love," he whispered.

She gave no reply. He wondered if he had pushed her too fast, if his great epiphany was not exactly shared.

But neither did she move or deny him.

Then he realized that he had found the words to say what he was feeling too late, at least for that evening.

Her breathing was soft and even, her fingers curled around his.

And she was sound asleep.

He smiled to himself.

It changed what he was feeling, deepened it, to know that she would sleep beside him, that they would wake together in the morning.

That he wanted to sleep this way every night of his life, and wake beside her again and again.

Would she feel the same? he wondered. Enough to really love this place, where predators roamed, the mosquitoes seemed elephantine and bit like crazy…and the sunsets were the most glorious man would ever see, and the birds that flew overhead came in all the colors of a rainbow.

He rose in the night and padded naked to the back window, looking out on the eternal darkness.

He heard her, felt her, before she came behind him, arms winding around his back as she laid her cheek against him.

Words failed him again.

He simply turned and took her into his arms. Though tenderness reigned, he found himself afraid.

Afraid to break the moment…

Afraid she didn't feel the same.

And later, still awake, he wondered if there was even more that had stopped him.

Fear…?

They had almost certainly killed the man-eater that had gotten Billy Ray.

They had not, however, captured the man who had created it.

Chapter 11

The massive alligator was being taken upstate for examination, but that didn't stop Harry Rogers from trying to use it to improve his tourist trade.

When Lorena arrived bright and early for work, she discovered that Harry knew how to move quickly. Out front, next to the ticket stalls, he had a mounted enlarged photo of the giant crocodilian—his own arm around it.

Lorena hadn't seen what had gone on overnight, so she was amazed to see that a number of the television stations had arrived, along with radio and newspaper reporters.

The monster was, as Harry and Michael had known, good for business.

The day moved rapidly, in a whirl of tours. Lorena took only a few minutes for lunch. Besides helping with the tours, she had to pull out an ammonia capsule to revive an elderly lady who stood in the heat a bit too long, patch up two little boys who scraped their knees, and treat an allergic reaction to a mosquito bite.

Michael was either too harried to bother her about the previous night or he had just gotten bored with the subject and didn't care any longer.

Sam and Hugh were both still a bit on fire, talking about the hunt the night before. Jesse had turned off his phone during the night, so Jack and Hugh, with Harry's blessing, were delighted to keep busy providing the reporters with what they needed.

The place was jumping.

The police waited until closing to make their appearance.

Lorena had just been saying goodbye to a group of tourists near the main entrance when she heard Harry's booming voice, alive with protest.

"A search warrant—for *this* place? What do you guys think that I'm doing here, feeding drug runners to my critters? What the hell are you after at an alligator farm?"

She noted that although a number of cops had arrived in vans with all kinds of equipment, Lars Garcia and Abe were the ones talking to Harry.

Lars sighed. "Harry, look, I'm sorry—"

"This is Jesse's jurisdiction, or so I thought!"

"Tribal law stands, unless the county, state or federal authorities have to step in," Lars said unhappily. He saw Lorena and studied her absently as he spoke. "Look, Harry, Jesse knows that we're here, and he's not feeling that his toes are being stepped upon. Harry, that was a monster they brought down. We have to search all the farms."

"For what?" Harry demanded.

"Evidence that someone's genetically engineering monster gators," Lars explained.

"What?" Harry seemed incredulous. "Look here, that was no creature from a horror movie. It was big, but it was just a gator. Jesse shot it, and it died."

"There has never been an alligator that size in Florida before," Abe said.

"There hasn't been one on record. Doesn't mean there hasn't been one out there."

"It was way beyond the norm, Harry," Lars insisted.

"Harry," Abe interjected, "God knows, you're an opportunist. Let's just hope you're not a crook."

Harry looked at Abe, enraged.

"Harry, please," Lars said, glaring at his partner. "Let us just clear you and your group so we can move on."

"You idiot!" Harry said, still glaring at Abe. "Clear me of what? Hell, am I an idiot? If I could manufacture a creature like that, do you think I'd let it out in the Everglades? Hell, no! I'd be making money on it."

Lars tried once again to explain. "Harry, we all know that a hatchling could get out. Someone could get careless, or someone could steal one, then lose it."

Harry threw up his hands, really angry. "You know what you can do with your search warrant as far as I'm concerned. But you go right ahead. You look into anything that you want to look into. Search yourself silly. I'm calling my lawyer. You know, if you wanted to see something at my place, all you had to do was ask."

Harry walked away muttering. Lars gave a slight smile to Lorena, shrugged and turned away to talk to a distinguished-looking man in a special-unit suit.

She hadn't realized that Michael had come up behind her. "The suspicious cops are your fault, I imagine?" he asked softly.

A shiver shot down her spine as he spoke. She spun around quickly. She didn't have to answer. He shrugged. "Not that I care. But if Harry finds out…mmm. You're in trouble. Big."

"Excuse me, Michael, I'm hungry," she said, and started for the cafeteria.

"I'm hungry, too," he said, trailing after her.

When they entered the cafeteria, Sally was rushing out. She didn't look at all amused. "Hey, sexy, what's up?" Michael demanded, stopping her.

She grated her teeth and cast Lorena what seemed like an evil stare, although she couldn't really be sure.

She might just be paranoid.

"They're inspecting everything, and Harry wants me there to explain the books. I don't get this—I don't get it at all! There was a giant alligator in the swamp—so we get *audited?* Not that there are any problems, I can assure you. My books are always perfect."

"I'm sure they are," Lorena murmured.

The woman might have been in a hurry, but she took time to glare at Lorena. "It's amazing, isn't it?" she murmured. "We were such a quiet place. Then you arrived and all hell broke loose. Did you have a nice time last night?"

"Yes, thank you," Lorena said evenly.

"What did you do last night?" Michael asked with a frown.

"Oh, come on, Dr. Preston! We have a budding romance in our midst, or didn't you know?" Sally asked.

Michael stared at Lorena. "You left with Jesse?"

"We're not required to stay on the premises," Lorena said.

"You're moving in with him?" Michael demanded. Lorena couldn't tell if he was angry or just surprised.

She looked at him incredulously, shaking her head. "That's kind of a leap, isn't it?" she demanded. She kept smiling, but the curve of her lips was forced. "This is my business, okay?"

"We're just trying to watch out for you," Sally assured her, suddenly saccharine. "I mean, well, you work here, so you're one of us. Jesse is…well, Jesse keeps his distance."

"Doesn't seem that he's keeping much of a distance now," Michael murmured.

"Hey!" Lorena protested again.

"Think of us as one big family," Michael told her.

"Okay, *bro*. I'm not moving anywhere. If such a thing ever happens, I'll be sure to inform my *family*," she said.

"How lovely," Sally murmured. "I'm off to see to my books. You children have a lovely dinner." She waved a hand in the air and left them.

"You know, you are going to have to tell us what's going on," Michael said, a hand at Lorena's back as he directed her toward a table.

She was saved from having to answer at that moment when Jack Pine joined them, sitting down with a weary grimace. "Busy day," he said.

"Oh? At your end, too?" Michael said.

"A bunch of scientist types, or so I'm told, will be in tomorrow. They want to investigate all our stock," Jack explained.

Michael stared at Lorena again. "How come I haven't heard anything about this?"

"Maybe they just haven't gotten to you yet," Jack suggested.

Hugh came over just then, settling down at the table across from Michael. "This is nuts."

"Are we closing tomorrow for all this?" Michael demanded.

"Oh, no. They can work around us. They're taking samples, bringing chemists and vets in, that kind of stuff," Hugh said cheerfully.

"It's absurd," Michael said indignantly. "I mean, my research is…well, it's *mine*. Where are my rights in all this?"

"I suppose the problem has something to do with giant alligators eating people," Jack said with a shrug.

"There are alligators everywhere," Michael protested. "Alligator farms abound in this state. Entrepreneurs run hunts on private property that aren't sanctioned or controlled by the state or federal government."

"Well, Michael, maybe they feel that your research will help them," Jack said. "Who the hell knows? Has anyone ordered dinner yet?"

Looking across the room, Lorena saw that Jesse had arrived. She was both startled and pleased, and jumped to her feet before she realized that despite the fact that their affair was growing obvious, she might have been a little more circumspect.

"Well, well," Hugh murmured.

Lorena ignored him.

Jesse was already walking over to them. He offered her a smile, held out her chair for her, then chose one for himself.

"So you reported Harry's as a hot bed of…what, exactly?" Michael asked.

Jesse frowned. "What?"

Michael leveled a finger at him. "Cops and the people from Fish and Wildlife are going to be crawling all over the place."

"I heard they're checking out a bunch of places," Jesse said with a shrug.

"Why assume that Harry's has anything to do with a giant alligator?" Michael demanded.

"Maybe because Harry sponsors a lot of research—
your research—into improving gator meat and hides?"
Jesse suggested.

"Can we order now?" Jack asked as one of the waiters
arrived at the table.

"Sure. We're in the middle of a criminal investigation.
Let's eat," Michael snorted.

"I'm hungry," Jack snapped back.

The tension was definitely growing, Lorena thought.

"Michael, they've got to find out what is going on,"
Jesse said. "There could be more of those creatures out
there. And if they don't find the sustenance they need in
the wild, that would put people in danger. "Come on, Michael. How many attacks on humans do you want to see?"

"There's no reason to think there are more alligators that
size out there," Michael insisted. "Maybe our gators are
just getting bigger all around, catching up with some of
their counterparts in other places. Maybe they should start
investigating that before they come out here on Indian land
and start poking their noses into things."

"Hey, this may be Indian land, but when it's a county-
wide problem—"

"The alligator was caught on Indian land, too," Michael
said testily, cutting Jesse off mid-sentence.

Lorena saw Jesse tense, but he wasn't the one who answered. "So what are you suggesting, Michael? That it's
all right because only Indians will be eaten?" Jack Pine
snapped.

"Don't be ridiculous!" Michael argued indignantly.
"I'm trying to be supportive of tribal law."

"Good of you to be concerned," Jesse replied.

"I think we should order dinner," Hugh murmured, nodding to the waiter, who had continued hovering in the background.

Fresh catfish was suggested and accepted all the way around. Most of the tension around the table eased, but a slight chill remained. Jesse seemed distracted, Jack stiff, and Michael annoyed. Only Hugh seemed oblivious to the general air of discomfort.

"So, any clues as to how our gator got to be such a monster?" Hugh asked Jesse.

"It's been sent off to Jacksonville. That's all I know right now," Jesse said.

"Hey, there's Harry," Hugh said. "He looks happy."

Harry, smiling broadly, breezed by the table. "Looking good, looking good," he told them cheerfully.

"What looks good?" Michael asked skeptically.

"This place. The phones have been ringing off the hook. People want to find out all about alligators. It's kind of like Jurassic Park meets the Florida Everglades. Hey, how's that catfish? Can't get any fresher."

"Harry, we don't know. We haven't got it yet," Hugh said, amused.

"Well, it's going to be great. We're on a roll, all of us. Keep up the good work."

Harry left just as their catfish arrived.

Lorena glanced at Jesse. Could Harry possibly be guilty of anything if he was this happy while the authorities were crawling all over his holdings?

Just as Jack remarked that the catfish was indeed excellent, a slender, balding man in a typical tourist T-shirt and khakis walked up to the table. "Dr. Michael Preston?" he inquired.

Michael sat back tensely. "Yes."

The man offered a hand. "Jason Pratt, Wildlife Conservation. Can you give me a few minutes of your time? When you're done eating, of course."

"I guess I'm done," Michael said, throwing his napkin on the table.

"There's no reason for you to rush," Pratt protested. "I just wanted to catch you before you retired for the night."

Since it was still early, it was unlikely that Michael had been about to go to bed. Maybe Pratt was afraid Michael was about to flee?

Michael rose. "No. I'm done. How can I help you?"

He walked away with Pratt. Jesse rose, as well. "Want to take a ride with me?" he asked Lorena.

"Sure," she murmured, rising, too. Jack and Hugh were exchanging glances. She knew that along with the giant alligator, she was definitely a topic of conversation between them.

"See ya," Jesse said, nodding, taking Lorena's hand and heading out.

"Where are we going?" she asked as they got into his squad car.

"To see Theresa Manning."

"Theresa Manning?"

"The woman whose friend was…eaten," Jesse said.

"And what are we going to learn from her?"

"I'm not sure, but I called to see if we could speak with her, and she asked us over for tea and scones."

"Tea and scones?"

He shrugged. "Apparently she likes to bake."

"Jesse…do you think Michael is behind all this? I had the strangest conversation with him last night."

He scowled fiercely, looking at her in the rearview mirror. "You were alone with him?"

She ignored that. "He seriously believes that I'm here to cause him trouble."

"You need to stay away from him."

"But if he's doing anything illegal…he's about to face the music, right?"

Jesse shook his head. "Someone else has to be involved. Someone with money."

"Harry has money, but he seems as happy as a lark."

Jesse's cell phone started ringing. He answered it, then fell silent, frowning. Finally he said, "Call me as soon as you find out anything."

"What happened?" Lorena demanded.

He glanced quickly at her. "The alligator never made it to the university. Somewhere between here and Jacksonville, the truck it was on disappeared."

Michael leaned against his desk, scowling as Pratt and the other investigators—ridiculously casual in jeans and cotton island shirts or T's—went through his research records and his computer.

"What's this?" one of them asked.

Michael came around and looked over his shoulder.

"A record of the temperatures required to create the different sexes," he said patiently.

"And what's this?"

"Maturity level for the most tender meat," Michael said.

"And this…?"

"Breeding for the best skins," Michael said wearily.

The man rose suddenly. Others were still working in the filing cabinets, but most of his records were on the computer.

"I guess that's it for now," Pratt said, smiling cheerfully.

Michael realized that he had broken out in a cold sweat. Now he felt a debilitating rush of relief.

They hadn't found anything. Nothing. Nada. Zilch. Not a damned thing.

"You're done?"

"Yep. Thanks so much for your time and your patience," the man said.

"Hey, uh…sure," Michael said. "Anything to help. Not a problem. Anytime. Come back anytime you think I might be able to help." He couldn't seem to stop himself from babbling, he felt so relieved.

Pratt thanked him again as he and the others left the office. Michael sank into his chair with a sigh of relief.

"Yeah, any time," he muttered. Then he looked at his computer and quickly logged into his secret files.

"Sugar? Milk? Lemon?" Theresa asked. "And…let me see. Those are blueberry in the middle, plain on the left side, and cinnamon on the right. I do so hope you enjoy them. I love to cook. My husband loved my cakes and pies."

Jesse had bitten into one of the blueberry scones. "It's wonderful," he told Theresa. "And it was so kind of you to make this offer. Delicious. Thank you. And for me, just tea is good."

"A touch of milk," Lorena murmured. "Thanks. And Jesse's right. These are just too good."

Theresa sat, beaming. "Well, I know you didn't come out for the scones. So how can I help you?"

"I know that this is painful for you, Theresa," Jesse said. "But you've heard all the ruckus about the alligator we caught last night."

Lips pursed, Teresa nodded grimly.

"Caught. It was caught," Lorena emphasized gently.

"That one was caught," Theresa said.

"So you think there are more?" Jesse asked.

"I think my friend was attacked by another one of your giant gators," Teresa said with assurance.

"Why?" Jesse asked her.

"They're territorial, aren't they? And yours was caught off the Trail. My friend was killed way out here."

Jesse cast a quick glance in Lorena's direction. "Was there anything strange going on at the time?" he asked Theresa.

"Strange?" Theresa repeated, then sat thinking for a while. "No. Nothing strange. Oh, now and then a few pets disappear, but…well, a small animal is natural prey, right?"

"I'm afraid so," Jesse said. "But you don't think there was anything else going on in the area?"

"Like what?" Theresa asked.

"Lights of any kind," Jesse said.

"Lights?" Teresa appeared confused. Then she gasped. "Why, yes, actually! There were lights in the sky several times right around the time when…" She paused, making a choking sound deep in her throat.

"Did they ever kill the alligator that took your friend?" Jesse asked. "Did animal control or the nuisance-animal division ever find the right gator?"

She shook her head, then returned to his previous question. "We had been joking about aliens arriving," she murmured.

By the time they left, Jesse looked grim. He was silent when they got back in the car, and silent as they drove. At last Lorena asked him, "So…you believe that several of these creatures have grown up in the Everglades, and that big money is behind it. Enough big money so that some-one is out in helicopters searching for their missing gators?"

"Yes," he said simply.

"But Harry is probably the one most involved with al-ligators who also has the most money," she said, lifting her hands in confusion. "And Harry is so happy he's practically singing!"

"We're moving forward," he said tensely. "The noose is tightening, and we will catch whoever we're looking for."

He didn't head back for the alligator farm but wound his way down the road that she would never have found her-self, the road that led to his house.

As he parked, he looked at her, arching a brow. "Stay here tonight?"

"I should go back," she murmured.

"No, you shouldn't. Ever."

She sighed. "Jesse—"

"You want to catch a murderer. Well, you've done all the right things. The authorities are involved now. You don't need to go back."

She decided not to argue with him for the moment.

As they got out of the car, she glanced his way with a small smile. "You really are in the wilds out here."

"Pretty much," he agreed, watching her.

"It's been a long, hot day," she said.

"And…?"

"And the last one in is…a fried egg, I suppose!" she said, and dashed toward the door.

She began shedding her clothing once she had reached the patio. And she was definitely the first one in the pool.

The water hit her with a delicious sense of refreshing

coolness. She swam from the deep end to the shallow, enjoying the cleansing of her flesh.

To her amazement, he was there, waiting for her, when she surfaced.

As she came up against the length of him, she was elated to feel the strength beneath the sleek flesh. His ink-dark hair was slicked back, and the green of his eyes seemed brilliant. His arms wrapped around her. "Skinny-dipping, Ms. Fortier? How undignified. Is this something you do frequently?"

She smiled and said softly, "Actually, no. This is the first time I've ever been skinny-dipping. In my whole life."

"I'm flattered. And honored."

He smoothed back a length of her hair, his lips brushing hers, hot and warm beneath the faint scent of chlorine. His arms tightened around her, bringing the full length of her body against his. Her breasts were crushed against the powerful muscles of his chest, her hips molded to his, and the perfectly placed thrust of his sex against hers was a titillation that thrilled and warmed her with a heady sense of anticipation.

"Does that mean," he asked huskily, "that the entire concept of sex in a pool is equally new?"

She started to answer, but his lips moved down the length of her neck and the words evaded her. He kicked away from the wall, the force slamming them more tightly together. She was scarcely aware of the slick feel of the tile steps when they landed there. For a breathless moment she met his eyes. Then she felt the full brunt of his body as he lifted her high against him, then thrust himself deeply inside her. She wrapped her limbs around him, and the fire that suddenly seemed to burn between them was an intoxicating contrast to the coolness of the water. She cast her head back, felt again the fury of his lips on her throat, breasts, the hollow of her collarbone…. Her lips met his again as they moved in the water, the night sky high above them, the whisper of the foliage around them, and the thunder of pulse and breath taking over. She buried her head against his shoulder as the power of need, and the agony-ecstasy of longing seemed to seep through her, spiral and grow, seize her and shut away the world. Her arms stroked his back; her fingers dug into his buttocks. She arched and writhed, and wondered that she didn't drown, but he kept them afloat, and in a cauldron of searing carnal mist until it seemed that the world exploded right along with the night stars, and she collapsed against him, still held tight and secure. Then she began to shiver, for the night, without the fire of him, was strangely cool.

"If I'd had any warning, we might have had towels," he said, amused, his lips handsomely curved as he pulled ever so slightly away.

"I was simply seized with overwhelming desire," she told him, and she smiled herself. "Quite frankly, I'm not sure I could have planned skinny-dipping."

"Stay, I'll get the towels," he said.

"But it's just as cold—"

She fell silent. He had already leapt out and, naked and dripping, headed for the house.

She realized that it was colder outside the water than in it, so she waited.

At first she eased her head back and simply smiled. She felt so wonderful that she refused to let herself wonder if she wasn't being a fool, falling in love with someone who made no promises, who was so distant.

But there wasn't a thing she would change, even if she could.

Her eyes opened suddenly, and she wondered why, aware that she was feeling the first twinge of unease.

She glanced around. Lights shone in and around the house, but beyond…

Beyond was the Everglades. Miles and miles of darkness and foliage and swamp, a land that was deep, dark and dangerous. A place where a million sins could be hidden.

She froze, aware then that she was in the light, that any eyes could be looking on from the darkness.

She was suddenly afraid, certain that the night could see.

"Here we are," Jesse murmured.

A towel was wrapped around his waist, and he had one for her in his hands. The sight of him seemed to turn back the darkness.

"Thanks," she murmured, rising, allowing him to wrap her in the soft fabric.

"Thank *you,*" he murmured, and kissed her lightly on the lips.

The brilliance of his eyes touched hers, and he repeated the words very softly and tenderly. "Thank you."

He lifted her up, and they headed for the house.

In his arms, she forgot the darkness, and any thought that eyes might have gleamed at her from the black void of the night beyond.

Chapter 12

Jesse was gone in the morning. So was his car.

And she was furious. Despite the night they had spent together, she had no intention of listening to him about not going in to work. She was in no danger at the alligator farm. It was alive with officials—local, state and federal. Nothing was going to happen to her while she was working.

She walked around, fuming, for several long minutes while she brewed coffee.

Just how long would it take to get a taxi out to the middle of nowhere? In fact, was it even *possible* to get a taxi out to the middle of nowhere?

Come to think of it, she didn't know exactly where she was. What did one say? Come out and get me. There's a dirt road off Tamiami Trail, and it looks as if it leads into nothing but saw grass and a canal, but there's really a house out there. Quite a nice house, actually. Swimming pool, state-of-the-art kitchen…

She swore aloud and hesitated, wondering if she should call in to work or just pray that Jesse would show up and drive her to work.

She pulled out her cell phone and stared at it, ready to put through a call to his cell, tell him what she thought of his high-handed tactics and demand that he come back immediately so he could take her to work.

He might, of course, simply refuse. He might even be involved in a situation from which he couldn't extract himself. Too bad. There were others on his day crew. He could send someone for her, and damn it, he *would*.

Just as she was about to punch his number in, her cell rang. Caller ID said the number was the office at Harry's.

"Hello," she said quickly, expecting Harry, though a glance at her watch showed her that she wasn't late yet.

"Hey" came a soft voice. Male.

"Michael?"

"No, it's Jack. We didn't see you at breakfast. We were getting a bit worried."

"We?"

"Hugh, Sally and me."

"That was nice of you, but I'm fine."

"Glad to hear it. Not that you shouldn't be," he said hastily. "Things are just a bit strange around here right now, you know? I mean, who'd ever think *I* would be in any real danger from an alligator? So…we were worried."

"No, I'm fine, just…" She hesitated for only a second. "Jesse seems to have gotten caught up in something. He's not here, and I'm afraid I'm going to be late."

"We'll come get you."

"No, I'm sorry. You don't have to."

"No, no, it's fine. One of us will come. Fifteen minutes."

Jack hung up.

She clicked her phone shut. The hell with Jesse and his high-handedness. She was running her own life. No matter how much she cared for someone, she wasn't going to be ordered about or dissuaded from her course.

Her father had been murdered, and she had never felt so close to capturing the killer. No way was she going to back off now.

Inside, she poured a last cup and turned the coffeepot off. And waited.

George Osceola reported on the missing van. It wasn't much of a report—the van was still missing. It had been on I-95. The driver had spoken to his wife at about ten-thirty in the morning, just after fueling up.

And then…

He and the van had just disappeared. County law enforcement throughout the state had been notified, along with the highway patrol, but so far, the van hadn't been spotted.

A call to Lars provided no further information.

Jesse looked at the phone and thought about calling Lorena. She was going to be really angry. But she hadn't called him to demand that he come back and take her in to work. Maybe she had fumed for a while, then decided on her own that the smart thing to do now would be to stay away from Harry's.

As he stared at his desk phone, it rang. A female voice greeted his ears, but not Lorena's. "Jesse, it's Julie. I was just calling in to see if…well, if anything else had happened."

"We're working on it, Julie, but I've got nothing to tell you."

He could sense her hesitation, then she said, "Jesse, I know it was probably foolish, but I went by the house last night. I mean, I have to go back inside eventually."

"I'd be happier if you'd stay away a little longer," he told her. "Just a few more days."

"A few more days," she echoed. "The police have asked me to wait a few more days, too. Before…before claiming the bodies. They're afraid the medical examiner might have missed something. But about the house…I'm going to need clothes."

"Julie, when you go, I'll go with you. And if you need my help at the funeral home or with the church…"

"It's all done, Jesse, thanks. I knew what they wanted," Julie said. "I didn't call you to cry."

"Sweetheart, you have the right to cry as much as you want," he assured her softly.

"Thanks, Jess, but what I need is to…to bug you and make sure no one stops until my parents' killer is caught. And also, I called because I keep thinking about the lights I saw out at the house."

"Plane lights? Helicopter lights? Men on the ground with flashlights?" Jesse asked. "What do you think?"

"I know they didn't come from anyone on the ground," Julie said. "To tell you the truth…I know why my mother thought aliens were landing. They hovered right above the trees. I didn't hear any noise. Of course, I was in the car, and they were at a distance."

"Thanks for calling Julie. I'll look into it. Trust me. I want to help you. I loved your parents."

"I know you did, Jesse. And they thought the world of you. So do I. And I'll wait till we go inside together, okay?"

"Perfect."

He hung up after a minute, then called Lars back. "We need to start checking the airfields. More specifically, we need to find out who has been taking helicopters up."

Lars groaned. "Every television and radio station out there has a traffic and weather copter! And when we were out at Hector and Maria's, you said an airboat had been through."

"So?"

"So we've been talking to a lot of people with airboats, Jesse."

"Yes, and that was a move that needed to be made. Now we need to find out about helicopters."

He heard an even louder groan.

"Lars, I keep hearing stories about lights wherever there's been an event with an alligator. You have more resources at your disposal than I do. Can you get on it?"

He heard the deep sigh at the other end, but then Lars agreed. "All right. I'm on it."

Satisfied, Jesse hung up. He drummed his fingers on the desk. Something had been bothering him, and he wasn't quite sure why.

He looked at the phone and thought about calling his house, then decided not to.

He rose suddenly, since he wasn't getting anywhere sitting at his desk.

He grabbed his hat from the hook by the door. "Where are you going?" George asked him.

"To check with Doc Thiessen on Jim Hidalgo. See if

anything else has happened over at the vet's. I'm pulling into his drive now, so call me if you hear anything," Jesse said.

Lorena expected either Hugh or Jack to show up at the rear of the property with an airboat. Instead, it was Sally who finally tooted her horn from the front. Lorena clicked the front lock and hurried out.

"Jesse's trying to keep you away from Harry's, huh?" Sally said.

"Why would he do that?" Lorena asked, hoping she wasn't giving anything away.

"Why? Killer gators, feds all over the place, something fishy in the air," Sally said with a laugh. "Actually, you should be happy. If he didn't care about you, he wouldn't be acting so much like an alpha dog. Well, maybe he's just the alpha-dog type. I don't know."

Lorena shrugged. "Thanks for getting me. I don't know what he got involved in, or when he might get back, but I don't like being late."

"Aren't you even a little bit worried about everything that's going on?" Sally asked her.

"Should I be?" Lorena asked.

Sally laughed. "Michael thinks you're a suspicious character."

"Michael is paranoid," Lorena murmured.

"Maybe. He's a scientist. Maybe all scientists get paranoid. They think their research is better than gold."

"Maybe it is. Sometimes."

Sally waved a hand in the air. "I don't think Michael has created a strain of giant killer alligators."

"Oh?"

Sally shook her head. "He always seems frustrated. He's a good-looking guy. I think he had the hots for you. Actually, until Jesse stepped into the picture, it kind of looked like you liked Michael."

"I like everyone at the farm," Lorena murmured.

"Just the slutty type, huh?" Sally queried.

"What?" Lorena snapped.

"Well, you *were* flirting pretty hard with everyone until you settled on Jesse."

Lorena stared out the front window. "Did you come to get me just so you could give me a hard time?" she asked.

Sally looked at her, eyes wide. "No! Of course not." A small smile curved her lips as she shook her head.

Dr. Thorne Thiessen wasn't in when Jesse arrived at the veterinary clinic.

Jim Hidalgo was there, though. "Hey, how are you feeling?" Jesse asked him.

"Fine. Just fine," Jim assured him.

"How come you're here? I thought you had the night shift? And where is the doc, anyway?" Jesse asked.

"This is the day he does calls. He covers a few of the alligator farms, you know. And he does cattle, as well. There are even a couple of folks with real exotics, snakes and things, and for them, he makes house calls. One day one week, two days the next. I guess it works for him."

Jesse chewed a blade of grass and nodded. "You still don't remember anything about what happened that night, huh?"

"Nothing. You still haven't caught the thief, huh?"

Jesse shook his head. "Tell me if I've got it right. You

were in the back, then…wham! And then nothing, nothing at all, until Doc was standing over you?"

"Yeah, yeah, then lights, sirens, cops, med techs… You know the rest. You were here."

"Right."

Jesse shrugged. "So when will the doc be back?"

"Tomorrow morning," Jim told Jesse.

"Where is he?"

"Don't know. He works lots of places."

"And you're in charge until then? What about the day guy?"

"He works with Thiessen, travels with him. Weird goose, if you ask me."

"Because he's white?"

Jim laughed, shaking his head. "Because he never talks. Hey, lots of folks live and work out here who aren't part of the tribe. We all get along. His day guy, though. John Smith. Who ever heard such a name for real? He's a big goon. Never talks."

"To each his own," Jesse said. "Thiessen must trust him. Anyway, you feel safe enough out here alone now?"

"I'm not alone."

"Oh?"

Jim gave a whistle. A huge dog came crawling out from beneath the desk where Jim sat. He was quite a mix. Evidently a little bit shepherd, chow and pit bull. Whatever else, Jesse didn't know, but it made for one big beast of a canine.

"I just got him," Jim said happily. "I call him Bear."

Bear wagged his tail.

"He likes you," Jim continued.

"I'm glad," Jesse said.

"Anyway, he makes me feel safe. He was sniffing and woofing before you got out of your car. When I told him it was all right, he sat right back down. Got him from the animal shelter."

"Great."

"Doc isn't too fond of him," Jim admitted. "But he knows I'm not happy anymore about holding down the fort by myself on the days he's gone and at night, so…" He shrugged happily.

Jesse nodded. "See you. Don't forget—"

"Yeah, I know the drill. If I think of anything, I'll call you."

"Yep. Thanks."

When he reached his patrol car, Jesse put a call through to the office.

The van with the alligator carcass was still missing. And nothing had been found of the samples taken from the vet's office.

There were no known leads on the murders.

He clicked off, hesitated, and at last called his house.

She wasn't answering. He hung up, then called back, and spoke when he heard his own message. "Pick up, Lorena, please. It's Jesse."

But she didn't pick up. She might have been in the pool, in the shower or in another part of the house.

Or she might have called someone to take her in to work.

He tried her cell phone.

She wasn't picking up.

Okay, so she was angry.

He put a call through to the alligator farm. Harry answered. "Hey, Harry. I'm surprised to hear your voice."

"It's still my place, you know. Despite the goons crawling all over it," Harry said. But he sounded cheerful.

"You just don't usually answer the phone."

"This place is doing twice the business we used to. No one here but me to pick up. The feds said I didn't have to close, just as long as they could go through what they wanted. Hell, they can go through anything, as far as I'm concerned."

"I'm glad you're happy, Harry," Jesse said. "I guess it would be tough for you to find someone to search the throng of tourists and find Lorena for me, huh?"

"Yes, it would be. But I can put you through to the infirmary, in case she's there."

"So you've seen her?"

"Not this morning. But I'm sure she's working, no thanks to you."

"What do you mean?"

"You're trying to seduce my help away from here, aren't you, Jesse Crane?"

"Harry—"

"Hang on, I'll put you through. How do you work this ridiculous, pain-in-the-ass thing?" he muttered.

Harry didn't put him through. He hung up on him. Irritated, Jesse snapped his phone closed.

His house was between the vet's and the alligator farm, so he decided to make a quick stop, see if she was there fuming and swearing at his furniture, then head out to the farm.

A sense of genuine unease was beginning to fill him. It was as if puzzle pieces were beginning to fall together, yet they didn't quite seem to fit.

He closed his eyes for a moment. Someone from Harry's was definitely involved. There had to be a money connection. And someone who knew the Everglades well.

There was more than one person involved, for sure. A connection through Harry's, a money man, someone with a knowledge of genetic engineering, and someone else, a hired goon.

Thoughtful, he picked up the phone to make one last call, then hit the gas pedal.

The phone rang, and Sally answered it.

"Hey," she said cheerfully. Then she glanced sideways at Lorena. "Sure… No… Yes, of course."

She clicked off, then offered Lorena a rueful smile. "Jesse," she said.

"Jesse?"

"Yeah, he wants me to make a quick detour."

"Uh-uh. No way. Let's go in to work."

"I think he's found something."

"What?"

"I think he's made a discovery. Something to do with… if I heard him right, your father."

"My father!" Lorena said, startled.

"Yeah. I didn't know Jesse knew your family. Hey, it's your call. He wanted me to bring you out to what they call Little Rat hummock. It's barely a piece of land, but they have names for every little hellhole and cranny out here. From the days when they were running and hiding out here, I guess. Anyway, what should I do? Jesse sounded all excited."

Lorena's heart flipped; her pulse was racing. She was still furious with him. But if had discovered something and needed her in any way, she had to be there.

"If Jesse were calling me," Sally said, sounding wistful, "I'd sure be going."

"I'm supposed to be working," Lorena murmured.

"Okay, we'll go to work."

Lorena lifted her hands. "No. Little Rat Hummock it is."

"Good thing I brought the Jeep," Sally said. "There's no real road out there."

There wasn't. Lorena thought they were going to sink in mire once and, if not, be swallowed in the saw grass.

But Sally knew the terrain. Right when Lorena was gritting her teeth, certain they were about to perish in the swamp, the wheels hit solid ground. Ahead, she saw a cluster of pines.

"You're not scared out here, are you?" Sally asked her. "You don't need to be. Well, maybe you should have worn boots, but don't worry—the snakes won't get you, not if you leave them alone. Besides here, in the pines, all you really have to worry about are the Eastern diamondbacks and the pygmy rattlers. Well, and the coral snakes, but they don't have the jaws to bite you unless they get you just right." She glanced at Lorena, who could feel herself turning pale. "Sorry. I'm out in the Everglades all the time, and I've never been hit by anything more vicious than a mosquito."

Sally brought the Jeep to a halt.

Lorena looked around.

There was nothing. Nothing but a patch of high ground, a bunch of pines and the saw grass beyond.

"I don't see Jesse."

Sally was frowning, staring ahead.

Lorena heard the noise, too, then. A throb of engines.

"Airboat?" she murmured.

"Yeah. What the hell…?" Sally murmured.

"It's probably Jesse," Lorena said, getting out of the car.

Sally got out, as well. She walked around the car, staring ahead, still puzzled.

"It's not Jesse," she murmured after a minute.

The airboat came around the cluster of pines that lay ahead. "It's Jack. Jack Pine," Sally said.

"So it's Jack. Maybe Jesse asked him to come out here, too," Lorena said.

But Sally shook her head. "No…no…something's wrong here."

Jack brought his airboat to a halt and leapt out.

"Oh, man," Sally murmured. She turned again. Lorena realized that they had walked some distance from the Jeep.

"Hey!" Jack called. "Hey, Lorena! Stop!"

Sally shook her head wildly. "Run!" she advised, and immediately took her own advice.

Lorena stared from Jack to Sally, then back again.

There was a large machete hanging from Jack's belt.

"Run!" Sally called back to her.

"Run where?" Lorena cried, chasing after Sally.

"Follow me. I know where I'm going!"

There were tire tracks in front of his house. Jesse hunkered down and studied them.

A Jeep. Harry's had a number of Jeeps. Any of the senior staff had access to them.

He checked the house quickly, but he knew the minute he entered that she wasn't there. He paused in back, though.

There were tire tracks in the front, but the broken foliage in back indicated an airboat had been by, as well.

At that instant, his heart seemed to freeze in his chest. He headed back for the car, already flipping open his cell phone.

"George, I've got Lars checking on a few things, and I've asked him to get men out here. But we know the area better than they do. I want everyone available out here. Something is going down *now*. Cut a swath from the vet's to Harry's, pie-shaped, fanning south."

"Jess, what the hell…?"

"Do it. Just do it."

Lorena stopped because she couldn't run anymore. Sally, ahead of her, had stopped, as well.

She looked back at Jack Pine, who'd been closing in on them.

Jack had stopped, too.

"What are you doing out here, Sally?" Jack demanded.

"Jesse called," Sally said.

Jack shook his head. "No."

"What the hell are you doing out here, Jack?" Sally demanded in return, sounding frightened.

"Following you. I saw the car from the airboat. I was on my way out to pick up Lorena, so I couldn't help but wonder why you were heading out there, too. What's going on, Sally?"

"Jack, you're a liar and a murderer!" Sally cried, her tone hysterical. "I couldn't let you get Lorena. I couldn't let it happen."

Jack shook his head, looking puzzled. "Lorena, get away from her. She must have been listening on the phone. She had to get to you before I did."

Lorena looked from one of them to the other.

Sally wasn't armed.

Jack was carrying one frighteningly big knife.

She had no idea where she was, only that she was far from the car.

"I have an idea," she said. "Let's all head back to the alligator farm and discuss this whole thing."

"Lorena, don't be ridiculous," Sally said.

Lorena realized that Jack was moving steadily closer to her.

"Get away, Jack," she said.

"Don't you get it yet?" Jack said.

"You're going to kill her—and me!" Sally cried. "Lorena don't you see? He's going to chop us up and feed us to his alligators."

"No!" Jack cried. "You've got it all wrong. You have to listen."

"Come on," Sally cried. "Lorena, move! One swing of that machete…"

"Lorena," Jack pleaded as he took another step toward her.

"This way!" Sally cried to her.

Lorena tried to maneuver around the three pines that separated her from Sally.

"No!" Jack cried. "No!"

He was coming after her.

She turned to run more quickly.

But as she did, she was suddenly running on air. There was no earth.

No hummock, no ground.

She was falling through space.

Falling, falling, into the darkness of a pit.

She hit the ground with a thud, but after a moment of breathless shock, she realized that she hadn't broken any bones. The ground was not hard. It was muck and mire. Of course. They were below sea level. It would be impossible to dig a dry hole.

She let out a sigh of relief, then heard the thud next to her.

Someone else was in the hole.

And then…

She heard the noise. Loud. A grunting sound, like a pig. No, not a pig. A huge, furious boar. Or…

An alligator.

Chapter 13

Jesse chose to take his own airboat, trying to follow the broken foliage across the Everglades, certain that time was of the essence. His heart felt heavy. There was so much ground to cover. The river of saw grass seemed endless. He'd already seen so much evil done out here. You could search forever to find a body.

No, he refused to think in that direction. She had to be alive. He was certain that Lorena had been lured somewhere, but where, he didn't know. Or even why. Except that she was a piece of the puzzle; she'd been the first to know that something very wrong was going on, and that they were talking technology.

Dangerous stolen technology.

They weren't going to find anything at Harry's Alligator Farm and Museum.

Because Harry wasn't guilty.

And if all went as the thieves had planned it, they wouldn't find the van or the alligator carcass, nor the specimens from Doc Thiessen's lab.

He still didn't have all the facts, but he was certain of one person who might be involved. And that person didn't intend for any of this to be discovered, and it wouldn't matter just how many people died. The frightening thing was that no matter how many people died, mysteriously or otherwise, the techno thief clearly believed he couldn't be caught. ·

Ahead, he saw one of the airboats from Harry's. And there was someone beside it, gesturing madly.

He cut his engine.

Sally.

"Jesse, Jesse! Help! Quickly. It's Lorena…. Help!"

His heart remained in his throat. "Lorena…?"

"Come with me. For the love of God, hurry. And be careful. It's Jack…he'll kill her!"

Jack? Jack Pine?

Sally was running. Jesse ran after her in a flash. She circled around the pines, then shouted to him.

"Hurry!"

He did. And then he plunged into the hole.

He should have seen it. Even concealed as it had been with bracken and brush, he should have seen it. Hell, this was his country. This god-forsaken swamp was his heritage. He knew it like the back of his hand. He should have seen the damned thing, and realized that it wasn't any natural gator hole.

No. This one had been dug intentionally. And it was deep. In the rain, it would flood. But in the dry season…

He landed hard. The hole was deep, and the thatch covering above kept out all but a hint of light.

"Oh, God, Jesse!" Lorena cried, recognizing him in the meager light. In a second she was next to him, warm and vital. He held her, damning himself a thousand times over. She'd come flying into his arms with such trust.

And he had no idea how to get them out of this mess. He pulled out his cell phone. No signal. Damn!

"Jesse?" Jack Pine moaned.

"What the hell?" Jesse said. He eased himself away from Lorena.

It was pitch black, and he wasn't a trigger-happy kid or a rookie, but Jesse pulled his gun, just in case.

"Stay where you are, Jack. I'm armed."

"I'm not your problem," Jack said.

Jesse blinked, trying to accustom his eyes to the eerie lack of light.

"Stay back," he said softly, his mind going a hundred miles an hour as he tried to figure out what the hell was going on.

Lorena backed up until she and Jack were both flat against the wall of earth and muck.

Above them, Jesse suddenly heard laughter.

Sally's laughter.

"What a pity I can't see you all down there. Sorry, Jack. You were really kind, likable. You shouldn't have been so determined to help Lorena. And Jesse...so gallant. See, Lorena? You were the problem. Everything was going just fine until you appeared. But it doesn't matter. They'll rip Harry's apart, but they won't find a thing. They'll just have to accept the fact that we've grown some big gators in the Everglades—and that they ate you all up."

She sounded as if she were happily reading a children's fairy tale.

"I have to go now. I have to get rid of both those airboats. Goodbye. Nice knowing you."

Jack exploded. "Dammit, Jesse. Do something. She's insane. I mean…she's not the brains behind things, I'd swear it, but when I realized she had Lorena, I knew something wasn't right."

It was then that Jesse heard it. The grunt…the grunt followed by the roar.

He'd been listening to alligators since he'd been a kid. He'd learned a lot about the sounds they made.

Those that had to do with mating.

And those that had to do with territoriality…and hunger. Or both.

"Hell," he muttered under his breath. He could barely see the other two. "Stay back," he warned them.

"Jesse," Lorena said softly. "What are you going to do?"

"I'm armed," he reminded her. But he was worried. Bullets at almost immediate range had barely pierced the tough hide of the alligator they had bagged two nights before.

He wanted to rush over to Lorena. He wanted to hold her, to place his body as a barrier between her and the creature in the darkness. He wanted to say a dozen things to her. He wanted to tell her that he loved her.

He stood dead still, listening, waiting.

The animal was moving. He heard it moving slowly at first, but he knew just how fast a gator could be.

Then there was the rush.

He spun, blinded, but going on instinct. He emptied the clip. The sound was deafening.

The animal bellowed and paused, then slammed into him. In the dark, he heard the jaws slam shut.

Close. So close that he felt the wind the movement created….

He jumped back.

"Jesse!" It was Lorena, shouting his name.

"Jack, we've got to straddle it!" Jesse yelled.

"Are you insane?" Jack shouted back. "These are monsters. They can't be wrestled down like a five- or six-footer."

"Do you want to be eaten?" Jesse demanded.

The animal had apparently been wounded, because it continued bellowing. Its senses were far better than his own, Jesse knew, but it seemed to be disoriented. He tried desperately to get a sense of its whereabouts.

Then he threw himself on the animal.

He aimed accurately, hitting the back just behind the neck. But the creature was powerful and began thrashing. Right when Jesse thought that he was going to be tossed aside like blown leaf, Jack landed behind him.

"What now?" Jack shouted.

"I've got to get on the jaws."

"I can't hold the weight!"

"You've got to."

"Wait! I'm here!" Lorena cried.

"Lorena, you don't—" Jesse began.

"We've done something sort of like this before," Jack panted. "Kind of."

There was a flurry of motion as the alligator gave a mighty bellow, tossing its head from side to side.

Lorena landed on the animal's back behind Jack.

"Now what?" Jack demanded.

"The jaw," Jesse said.

"You're mad," Jack responded.

"What? We can't ride this damned thing forever," Jesse said.

"But—"

"Big or little, if I can get the jaw clamped, we'll be safe."

"Yeah, yeah…if you don't get eaten first. Go for it."

He did. He had no choice. He tensed, feeling every inch of the creature beneath him, sensing with all his might, trying to ascertain what the creature's next twist would be.

And then he moved. He leapt forward, landing heavily on the open jaw, snapping it shut. The creature was mammoth; the jaws extended well beyond his perch.

He'd snapped the jaws shut, and still the animal was trying to fight him off. Its strength was incredible. It would shake them all off if they weren't careful.

Trying to maintain his seat, he reached into his pocket for a new clip. The animal bucked. He nearly fumbled the clip.

He tried again.

"Hurry," Jack breathed.

The alligator made a wild swing with its tail.

Lorena screamed. Jesse heard the whoosh as she flew through the air, the thud as she slammed against the mud wall of the pit.

The alligator bucked, fighting him wildly, beginning to get its jaws open, despite his weight.

"Jack, hold him!" he cried.

"Damn it, I can't. I can't!"

Then he heard Lorena, rising, breathless but as tenacious as the creature beneath him. "I'm coming."

"Watch it!"

The alligator swerved, knowing exactly where Lorena was, trying for her.

She moved like the wind, flying past him, landing behind Jack once again.

He could barely hold the gun, much less insert the clip. He had to. He had to, and he knew it.

He locked the clip into place.

He felt for the eyes, and he fired.

The ferocity of the bellow that erupted from the creature nearly threw him. The sound of the bullet exploding was terrible, almost deafening.

But he shot again.

And again.

At last the gator ceased to move.

For long, awful moments, none of them moved.

Jesse's ears were ringing when he finally said huskily, "Lorena, try getting up."

She did so, slowly, carefully.

The creature remained dead still.

"Jack."

Jack moved, but Jesse stayed. He groped around and found the base of the skull, then warned them, "I'm shooting again."

He delivered two more bullets into the creature.

Then, at last convinced that the creature had to be dead, he moved, too.

In the darkness, he felt her. But she didn't collapse against him the way a lesser woman might have. She strode over to him, and her arms wound around him as his wound around her.

Only then did she start to shake.

He heard Jack sink to the ground. "I think I'm moving north," Jack muttered. "Somewhere with ice and snow and no alligators."

Jesse allowed himself a moment to revel in simply holding Lorena, in feeling her, breathing her scent above the gunpowder and the muck.

"What the…?" Jack said suddenly. "Hell."

"What?" Jesse demanded sharply.

In the darkness, they could hear Jack swallow.

"What?" Jesse demanded again.

"There, uh, there was someone else down here," Jack said very softly. "There are…body parts."

"Oh, God!" Lorena breathed.

"Hey, we've got to keep it together," Jesse said sharply. "It's not over yet. We've got to get out of here. Quickly. They'll be back."

"They?" Jack said dully. Then he added, "Of course. They."

"Come on, Lorena," Jesse said. "I'll hike you up first."

He lifted her, and with Jack's help, he got her to his shoulders. From there, a shove sent her out of the pit.

"Hey! I found a big branch," Lorena called. "You guys can use it as a ladder."

She nearly hit Jesse in the head with it, but as soon as they got it in place, Jack reached upward, bracing against it. Jesse gave him a push.

They heard the tree limb cracking, but Jack was nimble for his size, and grasping for both the ground and Lorena's hand, he managed to throw himself to the edge of the pit. He turned then, ready to help Jesse. "Come on!"

Jesse eyed the height of the pit, the broken branch, and the length of Jack's arms. "Back off," he said.

"What?"

"Back off."

He gave himself a few feet, then ran at the tree limb, using it as a stepping-stone and no more.

He just made the rim of the pit, then hung there.

His grip slipped in the muck.

"Jack, where the hell are you?"

Jack didn't answer.

Jesse dangled. Then he got a grip, and at last, straining, he dragged himself over the rim of the pit. He rolled, then lay panting in the bright sunlight.

"Damn you, Jack," he said, turning.

And then he fell silent, knowing what had happened to Jack.

Both Jack and Lorena were still there. Completely covered in black muck and mire.

But the true killer, the thief, the one determined on getting rich at the expense of so many lives, had at last arrived himself.

Jesse made it to his feet, aware of the Smith & Wesson pointed at his face, and the grim features of the man he had once respected.

"Doc," he said. "Doc Thiessen. I've been expecting you."

"Damn, Jesse, why do you have to be so hard to kill?" Thorne Thiessen demanded.

"Hell, I don't know. I just like living, I suppose."

Sally was standing right behind Thiessen. Jesse noticed that she hadn't gotten rid of both airboats. There were two on the little hummock, his own and the one Doc had come in.

"So, Doc…I kind of figured you were involved in this," he said smoothly. He was playing for time now, but Doc didn't know that. Doc didn't know that the troops were already on the way.

"Oh, bull! You didn't have the least idea," Doc Thiessen said.

"Yeah, I did, Doc, but I was awful damn slow putting it

all together. At first I thought it was Harry, because Harry has money. But so do you. I admit, I didn't figure out right away who you had working for you, and I sure as hell didn't suspect Sally, but after I talked to Jim Hidalgo a few times, I knew you had to be involved. He gets whacked on the head, and the first one he sees is you. And those samples... You should have had them all prepared and studied and on their way somewhere else. You had to steal your own samples. And I'm willing to bet that by now Lars Garcia has found out that you own a helicopter, though I doubt you were the one flying it around, looking for your gators. That was probably John Smith. I'm willing to bet that the altered gators are marked somehow. They would have found out just exactly how if the one I shot had reached the veterinary school, as it was supposed to. I didn't suspect Sally at first, but I should have. She was the one who gave Roger a shove, wasn't she?

"So let me see if I've got it worked out. You were the leader, and Sally and John were working for you. Who did all the dirty work for you? The killing, Doc. Who killed Maria and Hector—and Lorena's father?"

"I really don't have time for this," Thiessen said, shaking his white head. The face that had always seemed so kindly was now twisted in a mask of impatience and cold cruelty.

"Come on. You beat me." Jesse tried to assess the situation. Doc was the only one with a gun, and it was now aimed at him. Jack and Lorena were standing to one side, where they'd been forced in the last seconds while he'd been getting himself out of the hole.

But neither Jack nor Lorena looked as if they were about to collapse. As if they had been beaten. They were survivors. Lorena had a steely strength to have gotten this far.

In fact, she looked both defiant and angry. She wasn't going to go down easy.

And he couldn't count Jack out, either.

Thiessen smiled. "Actually, you'll find out who does my dirty work in just a minute or two. But first I've got to decide how to do this. You killed my gator, Jesse. In fact, damn it, you've killed two of them."

"C'mon, Doc, what else could I do?" Jesse said. "But listen, since I'm going to die anyway, do me a favor. Explain it all to me first, will you?"

Doc shrugged. "Easy enough. Sally heard about the research, made the contacts and came to me, since she didn't have the expertise to work with what she'd found. I've worked my fingers to the bone out here, and you can't imagine the millions to be made off a formula that can create an animal this size. The old man up in his research lab panicked. He didn't have to die. But he found out I'd gotten hold of a few of his specimens. Found out that they were growing, and he didn't keep his mouth shut, the old fool. He had to go and confront me about it. He hadn't figured out Sally's role yet, but I couldn't take the chance he would. She'd worked for him briefly, and if she'd been caught, that would have led back to me. So he had to die. Just the way things go," he said coldly. "Now, as to Lorena being the old man's daughter, well, it took me a while to make the connection, I'll admit."

"You bastard!" Lorena said softly.

For a moment Jesse thought she was going to fly at Doc, but she controlled herself, tense as a whip.

Her eyes touched Jesse's. He realized that she was trusting him to get them out of this.

He couldn't fail her.

Thiessen was on a roll. "You should have accepted that accident, Ms. Fortier. The cops would have gone on believing that Hector and Maria had been involved in drugs. As to old Billy Ray, well, I didn't kill him. The old drunk ran into one my gators, that's all."

"Just how many killer gators are there?" Lorena asked tightly.

Thiessen appeared amused. "There were four. One died on its own—near Hector and Maria's. You killed two, Jesse. There's still one of these beauties out there somewhere, and trust me, I'll find it. I've had Sally eavesdropping all along, and as soon as there's word, I'll know. None of this was as hard as you're trying to make it look, Jesse."

"And getting away with it won't be as easy as you think, Doc," Jesse said. All he needed was a distraction. He was certain that Doc knew how to shoot, but he was no ace, no trained officer. A distraction, and…

He swallowed hard. Did he dare? He'd be risking Lorena's life. And Jack's.

Lorena was staring at him, waiting. She still seemed to trust in the fact that he intended to do something.

And if he didn't?

Then they could all be dead anyway, unless the cavalry got here pronto.

"Lars Garcia will put all these pieces together, Doc."

"Don't be ridiculous. Other people out here have helicopters, and airboats? They must number in the thousands."

"People who know reptiles as well as you do are harder to find," Jesse commented. "And I've already mentioned your name to Lars. What was it, Thorne? Not enough money in what you were doing, or not enough glory?"

"The world is changing, Jesse. Genetic enhancement is

being made on a daily basis. Clones are a dime a dozen now. You're got to be at the front of the flock."

"I'm telling you, Lars is on to you," Jesse said softly. "And you think that Metro-Dade Homicide will let go? You're out of your mind."

Thiessen looked troubled for an instant. "He has no proof."

"He will. I figure you marked those gators, tagged them in some way, and then let them loose on purpose, trying to see how they did in the wild. But you wanted to protect them from discovery at the same time, so you tracked them by helicopter, as well as by airboat. They're territorial creatures, so you probably shouldn't have let that one get so close to a populated area. That was a stupid-as-hell reason for Hector and Maria to die. Whoever killed Hector and Maria came on their property with an airboat. So tell me, Doc. Who did it?"

"I did," Sally offered, stepping around from behind Thiessen. "I did it, you fool. You thought I was nothing more than an attractive piece of ornamentation, a numbers cruncher. Background and nothing more. Well, get this. You underestimated me. You were friendly…you were even warm sometimes. But I could always see it in your eyes. I was nothing to you. But you were wrong. So wrong about me. I know how to be a mover and a shaker."

"And a killer," he said huskily.

She smiled. "And a killer."

She was slightly between him and Thiessen at that point. Jesse cut a quick glance toward Lorena and realized that her eyes were on him.

She was afraid, but not panicking. She would fight until her last breath. He had never felt such a connection to another individual in his life.

A diversion. He needed a diversion.

She was staring at him so intently, he was certain she knew what he needed, how to help.

He prayed.

Then he gave a slight nod.

"Hey!" Lorena cried.

Startled, both Sally and Doc turned slightly.

And he made his move. He threw his body hard against Sally's, slamming her into Thiessen, bringing them all down to the ground.

The gun went off. A scream sounded sharply.

Still smoking, the gun lay on the ground in Thiessen's hand. Nearby was a pool of blood.

Jesse slammed his fist down on the man's wrist, and Thiessen released the gun. Jack Pine stepped forward, kicking it far from the man's grasp.

"Lorena!" Jesse cried, and leapt to his feet. She was standing. Unhurt.

Unbloodied.

She rushed into his arms.

He held her, shaking, feeling as if the world itself had begun to spin madly.

"Get up," Jack Pine was saying harshly to someone.

Jesse pulled away from Lorena long enough to turn and look.

Thiessen was getting up.

Sally lay on the ground, her eyes open but sightless.

A hole in her chest was surrounded by crimson.

"Is it over yet, Jesse?" Jack asked.

Jesse let out a sigh. "Not exactly. I imagine that, in a few minutes, John Smith will be arriving. He'll have been alerted by now to the fact that we're out here. If he does show, he'll be picked up. And I would also say that within minutes half the Miccosukee force will be out here. They'll be followed by the Metro-Dade cops. I can hear the airboats now."

Lorena looked up at him, then down at Sally. She shuddered, but only for a minute. Then she spun on Thiessen.

"Who killed my father?" she demanded.

"Ah, that," Thiessen murmured.

"Who actually killed my father!" Lorena repeated.

"Not me. I didn't kill anyone." He paused, and Jesse could see his mind working, trying to find a way out, to make himself look less guilty. "Sally…the whole thing was her idea. That woman was bloodthirsty. I was beside myself when I learned about the death of your poor father. And Hector and Maria. If she hadn't killed them… But she was certain they knew something and would get Fish and Wildlife in."

"Rather than Metro-Dade homicide?" Jesse asked dryly.

"She was the one who forced me into everything," Thiessen said.

"Tell it to a jury," Jesse said.

"I intend to."

They heard the whir of an airboat motor coming closer. Jesse spun quickly, ready to dive for the gun if another of Thiessen's accomplices was arriving.

But it was George Osceola at the helm, and a number of tribal officers were with him. In seconds, they were rushing forward, shouting, going for Thiessen.

Seeing that the matter was in hand, George walked over to Jesse. "Everyone all right?"

"Except for Sally. She's dead," Jesse said.

"Sally!"

"Sally killed Hector and Maria," Jesse explained. "Were you able to pick up John Smith?"

"They're still looking for him. But, Jesse, you were right. Lars put out the APB, and Smith was spotted upstate. I'd bet money he abducted the van driver. We'll know more as soon as we get hold of him." George studied Jesse, then went silent. "Meanwhile, we need to get you all out of here."

"Hey!" Lorena cried suddenly. "Stop him! Doc's heading for the water!"

George Osceola swore; so did Jesse. They should have cuffed the man immediately.

Doc Thiessen was fast, and he knew the Everglades. He was tearing across the hummuck, heading for the water.

"Stop or I'll shoot!" George shouted.

Thiessen made a dive into the water. Jesse didn't think the man could make it—not with a trained force on his heels, several of them Miccosukees who had grown up in the area. It was a last desperate attempt at freedom by a desperate man.

They raced toward the canal. Thiessen had plunged deep, apparently hoping to surface at a distance, then disappear into the saw grass.

Jesse streaked toward the water himself, then stopped.

Everyone stopped behind him.

There was a thrashing in the water. Droplets splayed high and hard in every direction.

They were all dead still, watching the awful scene playing out before them.

Alligators were territorial.

And Thorne Thiessen had disturbed a large male in his territory. The dance of death was on.

There was no helping Thiessen.

He'd been caught in the middle of the abdomen, and now the mighty creature was thrashing insanely, trying to drown his prey.

Thiessen let out one agonized scream.

Then the alligator took him below the surface.

Gentle as dewdrops, the last glistening drops of water fell back on the surface of the canal.

And then all was still.

Jesse heard a soft gasp, but even without it, he had known she was there. He knew her scent. Felt the air tremble around her.

He turned, and her eyes were brilliant and beautiful and filled with tears. She had wanted justice, not vengeance, he realized.

It had been a fitting end to Thiessen, he thought himself. But maybe he needed to learn a bit more about mercy.

He took her into his arms. Felt the vibrance and life in her body.

He drew her tightly to him. And he didn't care about the tragedy they'd just witnessed, the mud that covered them both, or who heard his words.

"I love you," he said softly. "And it's going to be all right."

Epilogue

It was fall. The sun beat down on the water, but the air was gentle. Birds, in all their multihued plumage, flew above the glistening canal. Trees, hanging low, were a lush background for the chirps and cries that occasionally broke the silence.

There had been a picnic. A week had passed since the events at the hummock. They had all spent hours in questioning and doing paperwork for both the tribal police and Metro-Dade.

Michael Preston and Harry Rogers had both been horrified to discover that they had been under suspicion.

Hugh had merely been indignant that he hadn't been in on the finale.

They had all attended the funeral for Hector and Maria. Julie and Lorena were fast becoming friends, just as she was a friend of Jesse's.

Now, with the picnic cleaned up, with the others having talked over everything that had happened and finally gone home, Lorena stared out at the strange and savage beauty of the area and smiled.

Jesse, a cold beer in his hand, came up behind her, then took a seat at her side.

She leaned against him comfortably, taking his hand, holding it to her cheek. "There's one more monster out there," she reminded him.

"Yeah. We haven't heard any reports about it, but we'll arrange more hunts until we get it."

"And when you do…will you capture it or kill it?" she asked.

He smiled at her. "When an animal is altered, it's man's doing, not the creature's," he reminded her. "But these things could mate. Undo the balance in the Everglades. I don't like to make judgments, but if it's up to me…I think the creature is too much of a risk. Too many people have died already. Your father died to protect people from creatures like it, and so…"

"At least they didn't kill the van driver," Lorena said.

"They thought they did, though," Jesse said grimly. "John Smith thought the man was dead when he stole the carcass and drove the van into a canal. It's a miracle that he came to and escaped."

"Every once in a while, we get a miracle," Lorena said.

"So…" Jesse murmured.

"So…?"

"So somehow I doubt that you plan to keep your position at Harry's."

"I was thinking of doing something else."

"You want to leave," he said very softly.

"Actually, no."

"No?" His face seemed exceptionally strong then, handsome and compelling, his eyes that startling green against the bronze of his features.

She sighed. "I know it's soon, but I had been hoping you would ask me to stay here. My real love is the law. And causes. I'm great at causes, Jesse. It occurred to me that the tribal council could probably use a good lawyer now and then. And living here, with you…"

He laughed. "I love you. You know that. I have to admit, I've had my fears."

"You? Afraid?"

"This isn't just where I live. It's part of what I am. And you come from a world that's…glittering. Clean. Neat. Sophisticated. Not that we don't have our own 'Miami chic' down here, but…I'm not knocking anything, it's just that here…well, there are alligators in the canals. Water moccasins, and saw grass hardly stands in for a neatly manicured lawn. And my nearest neighbor is…well, not near."

She laughed softly. "Hmm. Water moccasins."

"I'm afraid so. Though they're not the vicious creatures they're made out to be. They're afraid of people."

"And alligators."

"Normally, they leave you alone if you leave them alone."

"Muck, mud, mosquitoes and saw grass."

"I'm afraid so."

She turned to him, touched his face. "But they all come with you," she said softly.

He caught her hand, eyes narrowing, a smile curving his lips. "Then you really would considering staying? I'd love a roommate, but I'd much rather have a wife."

Her heart seemed to stop. "Are you asking me?"

"I'm begging you."

She threw herself into his arms.

"Is that a yes?"

"A thousand times over."

He gently caught her chin in his hand, thumb sliding over the skin of her cheek. Then his lips touched hers. The breeze was soft and easy. The birds went silent. The night was as breathtaking as his kiss.

The wedding was a month later. They chose the Keys.

The bride wore white. The groom was dashing in his tux.

They were both barefoot, married in the sand at sunset.

They'd taken the whole of one of the mom-and-pop motels, as well as rooms in one of the nearby chains. The attendance was huge, with Seminoles, Miccosukees, whites, Hispanics and, as Hugh, the token Aussie, commented a bit of everyone in between. Even Roger had made it out of the hospital in time to attend.

The sunset was glorious.

The reception was the South Florida party of the year.

And when the night wound down, they were alone in their room that looked onto the ocean, feeling the gentle breeze, aware of the salt scent on the air…

And then nothing else, nothing else at all…

Except for each other.

* * * * *

Coming in September 2005 from

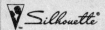

INTIMATE MOMENTS™

Hard Case Cowboy

by award-winning author

NINA BRUHNS

After a lifetime of bad luck, Redhawk Jackson had
finally hit the jackpot, working as the ranch foreman
on Irish Heaven. But when his boss's beautiful niece
shows up expecting to inherit his beloved ranch,
Hawk must decide what's most important—
his life's work or the woman of his dreams....

Where love comes alive™

If you enjoyed what you just read,
then we've got an offer you can't resist!

Take 2 bestselling
love stories FREE!
Plus get a FREE surprise gift!

Clip this page and mail it to Silhouette Reader Service™

IN U.S.A.
3010 Walden Ave.
P.O. Box 1867
Buffalo, N.Y. 14240-1867

IN CANADA
P.O. Box 609
Fort Erie, Ontario
L2A 5X3

YES! Please send me 2 free Silhouette Intimate Moments® novels and my free surprise gift. After receiving them, if I don't wish to receive anymore, I can return the shipping statement marked cancel. If I don't cancel, I will receive 4 brand-new novels every month, before they're available in stores! In the U.S.A., bill me at the bargain price of $4.24 plus 25¢ shipping and handling per book and applicable sales tax, if any*. In Canada, bill me at the bargain price of $4.99 plus 25¢ shipping and handling per book and applicable taxes**. That's the complete price and a savings of at least 10% off the cover prices—what a great deal! I understand that accepting the 2 free books and gift places me under no obligation ever to buy any books. I can always return a shipment and cancel at any time. Even if I never buy another book from Silhouette, the 2 free books and gift are mine to keep forever.

240 SDN D7ZD
340 SDN D7ZP

Name	(PLEASE PRINT)	
Address	Apt.#	
City	State/Prov.	Zip/Postal Code

Not valid to current Silhouette Intimate Moments® subscribers.

Want to try two free books from another series?
Call 1-800-873-8635 or visit www.morefreebooks.com.

* Terms and prices subject to change without notice. Sales tax applicable in N.Y.
** Canadian residents will be charged applicable provincial taxes and GST.
   All orders subject to approval. Offer limited to one per household.
   ® and ™ are trademarks owned and used by the trademark owner and/or its licensee.

INMOM05   ©2005 Harlequin Enterprises Limited

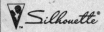

eHARLEQUIN.com

The Ultimate Destination for Women's Fiction

For **FREE online reading,** visit
www.eHarlequin.com now and enjoy:

Online Reads
Read **Daily** and **Weekly** chapters from
our Internet-exclusive stories by your
favorite authors.

Interactive Novels
Cast your vote to help decide how these
stories unfold…then stay tuned!

Quick Reads
For shorter romantic reads, try our
collection of Poems, Toasts, & More!

Online Read Library
Miss one of our online reads?
Come here to catch up!

Reading Groups
Discuss, share and rave with other
community members!

For great reading online,
visit www.eHarlequin.com today!

COMING NEXT MONTH

#1383 LIVING ON THE EDGE—Susan Mallery
Bodyguard Tanner Keane expected his assignment to rescue a
kidnapped heiress to be a no-brainer. And yet Madison Hilliard
wasn't at all what he expected. As passion sparked between them,
it was clear that his offer to keep her safe was anything
but. Would their combustible attraction stand in the way of
bringing down a deadly enemy?

#1384 PERFECT ASSASSIN—Wendy Rosnau
Spy Games
Her father was an assassin and after his murder, Prisca Reznik
took on a target list of her own for revenge. On her mission, she
encountered the very sexy Special Agent Jacy "Moon" Maddox,
who was responsible for her father's capture. Could the man she
meant to kill be the only man who could save her?

#1385 HARD CASE COWBOY—Nina Bruhns
No one ran faster from love than ranch foreman Redhawk Jackson,
until Rhiannon O'Bronach, his benefactor's niece, arrived and
made working together a necessity—and a sweet torture he'd
never envisioned. As they ran the ranch and dealt with its
hardships, Redhawk began to wonder if this tough-as-nails
woman was a threat to his future…or the key to his happiness.

#1386 WHISPERS AND LIES—Diane Pershing
Investigative journalist Will Jamison was sniffing out a story
that led him to an old friend. But little did he know the mystery
of veterinarian Louise "Lou" McAndrews's past would draw
him closer to her in every way. Not only had he stumbled upon
a secret that involved a powerful politician, but Lou's strength and
beauty made him rethink his vow to remain unattached. Could he
love her and keep her out of harm's way?

SIMCNM0805